"I think you got a pretty good look at me the other night."

"I mean, what's going on in here," he said, skimming his fingers over her forehead.

Pulling back decisively, she replied, "Not tonight."

"Did anyone ever tell you you're a damn frustrating woman?"

"No one who wasn't related to me. What about you?"

He shot her an indignant look. "What do you mean?"

"I mean has anyone ever told you that you're a damn frustrating man?"

He opened his mouth, then clamped it shut and narrowed his eyes.

"That can only mean one thing. So many people have told you that you're damn frustrating, you can't even count all of them."

"You're pushing for trouble."

"I already pushed for trouble. I've got a headache tonight."

He flashed her a seductive grin.

"Lady, I could make you forget your headache."

Dear Reader,

Top off your summer reading list with six brand-new steamy romances from Silhouette Desire!

Reader favorite Ann Major brings the glamorous LONE STAR COUNTRY CLUB miniseries into Desire with *Shameless* (#1513). This rancher's reunion romance is the first of three titles set in Mission Creek, Texas—where society reigns supreme and appearances are everything. Next, our exciting yearlong series DYNASTIES: THE BARONES continues with *Beauty & the Blue Angel* (#1514) by Maureen Child, in which a dashing naval hero goes overboard for a struggling mom-to-be.

Princess in His Bed (#1515) by *USA TODAY* bestselling author Leanne Banks is the third Desire title in her popular miniseries THE ROYAL DUMONTS. Enjoy the fun as a tough Wyoming rancher loses his heart to a spirited royal-in-disguise. Next, a brooding horseman shows a beautiful rancher the ropes…of desire in *The Gentrys: Abby* (#1516) by Linda Conrad.

In the latest BABY BANK title, *Marooned with a Millionaire* (#1517) by Kristi Gold, passion ignites between a powerful hotel magnate and the pregnant balloonist stranded on his yacht. And a millionaire M.D. brings out the temptress in his tough-girl bodyguard in *Sleeping with the Playboy* (#1518) by veteran Harlequin Historicals and debut Desire author Julianne MacLean.

Get your summer off to a sizzling start with six new passionate, powerful and provocative love stories from Silhouette Desire.

Enjoy!

Melissa Jeglinski
Senior Editor, Silhouette Desire

Please address questions and book requests to:
Silhouette Reader Service
U.S.: 3010 Walden Ave., P.O. Box 1325, Buffalo, NY 14269
Canadian: P.O. Box 609, Fort Erie, Ont. L2A 5X3

LEANNE BANKS

PRINCESS IN HIS BED

Published by Silhouette Books

America's Publisher of Contemporary Romance

SILHOUETTE BOOKS

ISBN 0-373-76515-0

PRINCESS IN HIS BED

Copyright © 2003 by Leanne Banks

Printed in U.S.A.

Books by Leanne Banks

LEANNE BANKS,

a *USA TODAY* bestselling author of romance and 2002 winner of the prestigious Booksellers' Best Award, lives in her native Virginia with her husband, son and daughter. Recognized for both her sensual and humorous writing with two Career Achievement Awards from *Romantic Times,* Leanne likes creating a story with a few grins, a generous kick of sensuality and characters that hang around after the book is finished. Leanne believes romance readers are the best readers in the world because they understand that love is the greatest miracle of all. Contact Leanne online at leannebbb@aol.com or write to her at P.O. Box 1442, Midlothian, VA 23113. A SASE for a reply would be greatly appreciated.

This book is dedicated to all my royally wonderful
readers who wanted Michelina's story.
You're all princesses in my eyes.

Prologue

The wig was going to change her life.

Michelina could barely contain her excitement as she pulled off her tiara and covered her black hair with the dull brown wig. She'd already scrubbed her face free of her usual cosmetics and changed out of her chic designer dress into an unremarkable skirt and blouse she'd filched months ago from her new sister-in-law, Tara York Dumont.

Everyone had remarked on how Michelina had transformed Tara's wardrobe and sense of style. They didn't realize that all the while Michelina had been quietly taking lessons from Tara and observing the advantages of being a plain woman. Everyone noticed a glamorous, beautiful woman, but a plain woman disappeared, which was exactly what Michelina intended to do. Of course, Tara hadn't really been plain.

She'd just dressed herself unbecomingly to disrupt her father's matchmaking attempts. Michelina's brother Nicholas had seen straight through Tara's ploy, and the two of them had quickly learned they were soul mates.

Sweet, Michelina thought, rolling her eyes, but she had lots of life she wanted to live before her mother, queen of the island country of Marceau, succeeded in marrying her off to Count Ferrar of Italy.

Michelina made a face at the mirror in the powder room of her cousin's house in Paris. Music from the party vibrated off the walls. She put in the tinted contact lenses she'd ordered from the Internet along with her fake passport. Another observation from Tara. Amazing what a girl can order off the Internet to alter the color of her distinctive silver eyes to brown, and her heart raced at her reflection. She didn't even recognize herself!

Shoving her fake passport and the rest of her belongings into her reversible bag, Michelina took a deep breath, left the bathroom and wound through the throng of guests. Her bodyguards stood next to the front door. She knew their instructions were not only to protect her, but also to keep her from running away. Michelina had nearly bitten her tongue off at least a thousand times during the last month in order to persuade her mother to allow her to attend her cousin's party.

Reaching the front door, she leaned close to the housekeeper so she wouldn't be overheard. ''I need some air,'' she said.

The housekeeper opened the door. "Of course, mademoiselle."

"Merci beaucoup," Micheline thanked her, and slipped out the door. Her heart hammering a mile a minute, she forced herself to walk down the hall, then down the stairs. Luck was in her favor. The doorman caught a cab for her right away. Her muscles pulled tighter than an overstretched rubber band, she knew she wasn't nearly free yet. At Charles de Gaulle Airport, she made the endless trek through security, her palms sweating all the while. What if they found out her passport was fake? What if they pulled off her wig?

But her fears proved unfounded, she finally boarded the jet and took her seat, her first time in coach. She thought of her brother Nicholas and his wife, Tara, her oldest brother Michel and his wife, Maggie, and felt a stab of guilt. They would worry. Then she remembered the secret they'd kept from her. Her anger and resolve flared like a wild fire.

They'd thought she couldn't handle the news that the brother they'd long believed dead was in fact alive in the United States. She would prove them wrong. She would go one better. She would find him and bring him back. She would prove once and for all that she wasn't Princess Useless.

The jet began to move faster, the engines roared and the force of the takeoff pushed her back against her seat. Euphoria shot through Princess Michelina Dumont. She had escaped.

Her mind was already in America. First stop: Wyoming.

One

Princess Michelina had bought herself a black Ford truck.

Exhilaration at her newfound freedom, however, was tempered with a sliver of uneasiness. She was somewhere in Wyoming, but she wasn't exactly sure where, and she had a sinking sensation she should have purchased a mobile Global Positioning System.

The skinny road wound through the darkness with a few token signs. It was bad enough that she didn't know where she was, but Michelina constantly had to fight the urge to veer to the left side of the road.

Why did Americans drive on the wrong side of the road, anyway?

She turned a corner, and her headlights flashed across a cow standing in the middle of the road. Panic sliced through her. She veered to the right and barreled through a fence. Before she could catch her breath or regain control of the truck, a barn loomed in front of her. With a cry of panic, Michelina slammed on the brakes.

Too late. She plowed into the barn. The last thing she saw was the steering wheel before her head slammed into it. Everything went black.

"Truck hit the barn! Truck hit the barn," Gary Ridenour yelled as he burst into the foyer of Jared McNeil's quiet home.

Jared kissed his chance for an hour of evening peace goodbye and stuffed the newspaper into the magazine holder as he stood. He fought an undertow of dread. "What do you mean, 'truck hit the barn'?"

Breathless from his sprint, Gary shrugged and waved his arms. "Some truck came out of nowhere and ran into Romeo's barn."

Alarm sliced through Jared and he immediately grabbed his keys and headed for the door. "Romeo!" Romeo was his prize bull, and raked in the bucks with stud fees. Jared stomped through the front door and down the steps with Gary at his heels. "What happened?"

Gary shrugged again. "I'm not sure. I thought about checking on Romeo, but decided I'd better come and get you first."

Jared nodded and climbed into his truck. "Damn, if anything happened to that bull, whoever ran into the barn is going to learn the meaning of the word *trouble*."

Gary scooted into the truck just as Jared started the

engine, shooting his boss a wary look. Everyone knew how important Romeo was. "That bull's tough. Maybe he slept through the whole thing."

"Romeo's a big baby," Jared corrected, scowling as he turned onto a dirt road. "He's probably bawling his head off."

Jared didn't need this. Besides being the owner of the largest ranch in southeastern Wyoming, he was interim everything at the moment. The local mayor had quit ranching and retired to Florida, so Jared was filling in until someone's arm was twisted hard enough to persuade him or her to take on that position, and since his sister and her husband were recovering from a serious automobile accident, Jared was filling in as caretaker to his two young nieces. Rounding the curve in the road, he pulled to a sharp stop and stepped out of the truck.

The night was black as pitch, and the first sound Jared heard was a bull bawling for all he was worth. Just as he'd predicted. He scowled. "I guess that's a good sign. At least he's not dead," he muttered as Gary joined him and they walked into the barn.

Romeo was alternately pawing the ground and bawling as he lifted his head toward a black truck in the barn. Jared felt a sliver of relief that his prize animal appeared to be physically unharmed. Ready to tear a strip off the reckless driver who'd crashed into the barn, he walked toward the truck. "Hey, buddy!" he called. "You better have damn good insurance—" He broke off when he saw a woman slumped over the wheel. Swearing under his breath, he pulled the door open. "What the—"

Gary raced to his side. "What is it, Mr. McNeil? What…?" Gary gawked. "It's a lady."

Jared tentatively reached out to touch the woman, and she moaned, sending a trickle of relief through him. "She's alive," he murmured. "Miss?" he asked, reaching for her hand and patting it.

"Should we call 911?" Gary asked.

"Let's give it another minute or two," Jared said, still patting her hand.

She lifted her head slightly and moaned again. *"Mon dieu,"* she said under her breath.

Jared couldn't hold back a wince at the furrow of pain between her dark eyebrows. Her dark silky hair sweeping over her cheek couldn't conceal her finely sculpted bone structure and velvet-textured, tanned complexion. Her eyelids fluttered, her eyes slowly focusing on him.

The intense, light-gray, almost silver color of her eyes took his speech for a full moment. He blinked, and of its own volition, his gaze traveled down the rest of her. She wore a fitted T-shirt that emphasized her small, round breasts and didn't quite meet the top of the low-slung jeans that hugged her hips and long legs.

Her eyelids fluttered again, and her dark eyelashes provided a sexy peek-a-boo fringe that concealed her exotic eyes.

Jared inhaled and caught a whiff of a scent that combined French, forbidden and expensive. He had the uncomfortable feeling that this woman was going to be trouble.

"Are you okay?" he asked.

She nodded slightly, then winced. "I think so, but my head hurts like bloody hell."

Trying to place her accent, which had traces of French, British and American, he pointed his finger at her forehead. "You're going to have a goose egg."

She glanced past the steering wheel. "What about the damage? How bad is the damage?"

"I think the bull will be okay, but you knocked out most of this side of the barn."

"I was referring to my truck," she said in a regal tone.

Jared raised his eyebrows. "I haven't inspected your truck. As long as you have good insurance, you should be okay."

She looked at him with a blank gaze, and Jared felt his stomach sink. No insurance. He would bet half his acreage on it. He narrowed his eyes. He was done helping wealthy damsels in distress. If Miss Silver Eyes didn't have insurance, then she could fork over the money. "I'm Jared McNeil and this is my barn and my ranch. What's your name?"

"Mi—" She broke off, and a sliver of panic crossed her face.

"Mi—what?"

"Mimi," she said with conviction.

"Mimi what?"

She paused a half beat, her gaze flickering away from his. "Deer—" she looked at him again "—man. Deerman. Mimi Deerman. Please accept my apologies for running into your barn."

She said it with such smooth expectancy that he almost nodded and said of course. But he caught himself. "The insurance company can handle the official apology. Are you from around here? Is there someone we can call?" he asked, even though he already knew the answer.

She shook her head, wincing slightly again.

He felt a small measure of sympathy for her. It was dark, she was lost...without insurance. His blood pressure spiked, and he pushed the thought aside. "Do you want to go to the hospital?"

Her eyes widened in panic. "Oh, no. I'm fine," she said, slowly stepping from the truck. "I just need—" She broke off, and the color drained from her face.

Jared automatically caught her against him. "Are you sure you don't want to go to the hospital?"

"Absolutely," she insisted. "Maybe I could just sleep in the truck."

Gary made a clucking sound. "You can't let her sleep in the truck, not with a hurt head."

Jared swallowed a growl of frustration. "I've got an extra room. You can stay at the ranch. Just for the night," he said for everyone's benefit, including his own.

"I'm greatly indebted to you." She met his gaze and he felt the punch of emotional fire in his gut. Like heartburn. He wouldn't be a man if a vision of her expressing her gratitude in dark, forbidden ways didn't cross his mind.

He cleared his throat. "It's just a night's sleep. We'll settle the score on the insurance in the morning."

Her face paled again, and he lifted her off her feet.

"Gary, see what you can do about securing the barn for the night. Move Romeo to one of the other barns. We'll take care of this mess in the morning."

Carrying her soft, curvy body to his truck, he tried not to inhale her man-trapping scent, and steeled himself against the temptation to take another slow, leisurely glance down her lithe, inviting form. Once upon a time, his sister had diagnosed his problem with women, and Miss Mimi's collision into his life just proved the point. According to his sister, Gina, Jared was a chaos magnet. He attracted women bent on wreaking chaos on his world and the world at large. One look at Mimi Deerman, and he knew she would give new meaning to the term.

The sounds of shrieking demons vibrated inside Michelina. Squinting her eyes, she winced at the obscenely bright light filling the room. She put her hands over her ears and slid her aching head underneath the pillow. Who on earth was screaming? Her mother would lay a Fabergé egg at such a disruption in the palace.

Michelina rubbed her cheek against the pillow. Something about the texture felt different. She peeked out from under the pillow. She wasn't in the palace, she recalled, her head still pounding like a cannon firing a ceremonial salute. She was in Wyoming.

Excitement and apprehension knotted her stomach as the previous evening's events came back to her. Her truck, she thought, frowning. She needed to get it repaired so she could continue her search for

Jacques. Slowly rising, she thought of the man who had carried her to his home.

Obligatorily kind, attractive if a woman preferred the overbearing, alpha-male type. Which she didn't, she thought, rolling her eyes. Her family was full of overbearing males.

The door to her bedroom burst open, and two little girls raced through, with Jared McNeil and a barking dog on their heels.

"Don't! Katie! Lindsey!" He finally stopped them when he grabbed them by the backs of their nightgowns. "I told you—" He broke off when he caught sight of Michelina sitting up in bed.

"Who's she?" the older child asked.

"She's here—" he hesitated briefly, then went on "—because she had car trouble and she got stranded last night. She's leaving today."

Michelina raised her eyebrows at his muddy explanation. "Car trouble. My truck—"

"Mimi Deerman," he interrupted loudly, "meet Katie and Lindsey, my nieces. They're staying with me while my sister and her husband recover from injuries they received—"

"—in a real bad car crash," Katie said, with worry in her young eyes.

Realization hit her. Mr. McNeil's altering of the facts was his attempt to be sensitive to his little nieces' situation. Her estimation of him climbed a notch. "Oh," Michelina said. "It's my pleasure to meet you. I'm very sorry to hear of your parents' accident."

Katie looked up at Mr. McNeil. "She's pretty, but she talks kinda funny."

He shrugged in agreement, then steered the girls toward the door. "Helen has oatmeal waiting for you at the table. Come on, Leo," he said to the dog, and tossed a glance over his shoulder. "You and I can settle the insurance matter in a few minutes."

Michelina froze. *Insurance?* Catching Mr. McNeil's intent gaze, she smiled to hide her panic. "No problem. After all, how much can a barn wall cost?"

Thirty minutes later, Michelina nearly fell out of the leather chair on which she perched in Jared McNeil's home office. She shook her head in dismay. "A barn wall *can't* cost that much."

"That doesn't include the repairs to your truck."

"The repairs can't be very expensive. It's just the front of the truck."

He gave her a pitying glance. "You'd be amazed what bodywork costs."

She opened her mouth to protest, but Jared's two nieces burst through the door. "Helen fell and she says she can't walk on her ankle!" Katie said.

"Helen?" Michelina echoed.

"Helen's my housekeeper. She was asleep when I brought you in last night," Jared said as he stood. "Where is she?" he asked Katie.

"At the bottom of the basement stairs."

"We'll finish this in a few minutes," he said to Michelina. "Whoever said trouble comes in threes was wrong," he muttered as he left the room. "My troubles come in *tens*."

Michelina felt a modicum of sympathy for the man.

Between the responsibility of his nieces, Michelina's untimely entrance into his barn, and Helen's fall, she could see that things definitely weren't going his way. She, however, had her own concerns. Michelina had brought enough money to live comfortably for one month, and then the truck had cost a little more than she had planned. She couldn't draw additional money from her account because it would be traced to her, and her one shot at independence would be over before she'd experienced anything. She felt her confidence begin to deflate like a balloon. What if what they said was true? What if she was too flighty to take care of herself or anything of importance? What if she really was Princess Useless?

The questions stabbed at a secret part of her she kept hidden. A princess wasn't supposed to suffer a lack of self-confidence, and if she did, God forbid that she expose it. At the thought of returning to Marceau, Michelina's stomach began to knot and burn. It seemed as if it had been knotting and burning more frequently during the last year.

Closing her eyes, she took a deep breath and tried to assure herself. She'd just got started. Sure, she had hit a bump in the road, technically a barn, but that didn't mean she had to abandon her plan. She would just need to improvise.

Jared McNeil appeared in the doorway, raking his fingers through his thick dark hair. "Do you know anything about kids?" he asked doubtfully.

The skepticism in his dark gaze rubbed at a raw spot. She'd seen the same expression on her brothers' and mother's faces. "Of course I do," she said, and

rationalized that she did have nieces and a nephew…
and she had once been a child herself after all.

"I wouldn't normally do this, but I think Helen has
broken her ankle, and that means I've got to get her
to the clinic so it can be treated. I don't want to take
the girls," Jared explained.

"I can take care of them," she offered impulsively.
How hard could it be? His two nieces seemed like
sweet children.

"You're sure?"

"Quite sure," she said, irritation bleeding into her
tone as she stood to make herself feel more equal to
him. It didn't quite work since he was still at least
six inches taller. She lifted her chin to compensate.

"Well, I'm stuck, so you'll have to do. I'll give
you my cell phone number in case you run into trouble. You might have to fix their lunches."

Michelina blinked. The palace staff hadn't allowed
her near the kitchen since the cake she'd attempted
to bake had exploded in the oven.

He sighed as if he'd read her mind. "PBJ sandwiches will do."

She refused to allow him to believe she didn't
know what PBJ sandwiches were. "I'm sure they
will."

"Katie can help you if you get in a bind."

Michelina narrowed her eyes. Now that was *in-
sulting*. "How old is Katie?"

"Five, but she likes to help in the kitchen. Something tells me you haven't spent a lot of time there,"
he muttered, pulling a card from his desk and pointing

to a number printed on the business card. ''Call if you have any problems at all.''

''There won't be any,'' she assured him, reaching for the card.

''I want your word,'' he said, holding on to the card.

She met his gaze and felt indignation mingle with a strange desire to meet his challenge. Michelina sensed this man was everything she wasn't—confident in himself and his abilities, accomplished, successful. She envied him all those qualities and was determined to get the same for herself.

''I give you my word of honor,'' she said quietly, meeting his hard gaze without flinching.

She saw a snap of electricity flicker through his dark blue eyes, and it filled her with a heady sensation, like drinking one too many glasses of champagne. His sexual intensity caught her off guard, and she couldn't make herself look away.

He pressed the card into her hand, and the touch of his warm, calloused palm made her nerve endings jump. For a few seconds, she wondered if he would be just as confident as a lover. She had a sneaking sensual suspicion that Jared McNeil knew how to motivate a woman to take care of his needs and how to take care of hers with breath-robbing ease.

An internal warning bell clanged, and Michelina took a mental step back. That blow to her head must have affected her thinking ability. She would examine her response later, she thought, pushing aside a tinge of uneasiness. He was just a man, she told herself. She would watch over his nieces this morning, be on her way this afternoon and forget him by evening.

Two

She could speak four languages fluently and had graduated from college with honors. She had been taught the names of the heads of state for every country in the world.

Why hadn't anyone bothered to teach her how to change a diaper? The palace nursery aides had always taken care of that particular task.

Lindsey would celebrate her third birthday in six months, but she wasn't ready to leave the world of diapers. It was humiliating, but Katie coached Michelina through the task. She just hoped the diaper wouldn't fall off. In her effort to avoid making it fit too snugly, she might have erred too far in the other direction.

Lunch followed and Michelina scowled as she remembered Jared's suggestion that she might need help for that task, too. If he hadn't abbreviated the name of the sandwich, she wouldn't have had a problem. Even she could spread peanut butter and jelly on slices of bread.

After lunch, she read approximately eighteen books in hopes of coaxing the girls into taking a nap. No such luck. Desperate, she played dress-up with the girls, applying lipstick and nail polish, fixing their hair and allowing them to take turns wearing the tiara she'd stuffed into her bag at the party when she'd escaped.

When Jared walked through the door with Helen, a middle-aged woman wearing a cast and walking on crutches, Michelina was pleased that she had delivered on her promise.

He didn't look pleased at all.

"I can probably still cook," Helen was saying, "but I don't think I'll be able to keep up with the girls while I'm on crutches."

"No, you won't, and finding someone is going to be—" He broke off and raked his hand through his hair.

Helen glanced at Michelina and gave a weary smile. "I don't believe we've met. I'm Helen Crosby. Jared told me about you. Mimi, is it?"

"Yes, it is. A pleasure to meet you. I'm so sorry about your fall. Perhaps you should sit down and rest—you've had a terrible day."

Helen glanced at Jared. "She's lovely," she said in surprise, making Michelina suspect Jared hadn't described her in flattering terms.

She studied his face, but he'd plastered a blank

expression on his tough features. Michelina was no fool. She'd seen her brothers don the same expression too many times to count.

"Let's get you to your room," he said gruffly to Helen.

"Maybe," Helen began thoughtfully, "maybe Mimi would be willing to care for the children."

Jared and Michelina shook their heads with equal fervor.

"Oh, no," Michelina said.

"No chance," Jared said at the same time.

Although Michelina was in full agreement, his tone grated on her.

Helen shrugged. "Well, it's bound to take a week or more to get her truck fixed, so she's got to stay somewhere."

But not here, Michelina thought.

"Not here," Jared said aloud.

She frowned, annoyed again by his tone.

"And you mentioned there might be a problem with her insurance," Helen added gently. "Maybe you could work out the barn damage in trade."

"Trade!" Michelina echoed.

"I don't think she's qualified," Jared said flatly.

"I could supervise," Helen said, then sighed. "You were right, Mimi. I think I need to go lie down. I'm sure you two will settle this in everyone's best interest."

Michelina's mind turned upside down as Jared helped Helen to her bedroom. She paced the length of the den as she whispered to herself, "Child care? Trade? This is ridiculous. How am I supposed to be independent if I stay locked up here? Surely, it would be better to be captive on Marceau than—''

Jared strode back into the room and pinned her with a gaze that stopped her words and stretched her nerves. ''Do you have insurance or not?''

Michelina swallowed over a sudden knot in her throat. ''I had just purchased the truck and hadn't quite—''

''Just what I thought,'' he said, interrupting her. ''No insurance. How do you plan to pay for damages?''

She bit her lip as he moved toward her. She wasn't accustomed to people invading her personal space without her permission. ''Well, I can pay for the damages. Just not now.''

''When?''

She cleared her throat. ''Perhaps a month. Or two.''

He stared at her in amazement. ''You think I'm going to accept an IOU from *you?*''

Insulted, she opened her mouth to protest, then remembered she was operating under an assumed name. The man was, unfortunately, justified in not trusting her. ''I had hoped.''

His jaw hardened and he shook his head slowly. ''No way. I'm not taking it in the wallet again for a pretty face. We'll go with Helen's suggestion. You can work off your debt to me in trade. Helen will supervise you.''

Shock raced through her. *''Supervise me!''* she echoed, nearly bursting with indignation. ''I never—''

''I thought so,'' Jared said, interrupting her again.

"I thought you didn't have much child care experience. That's why Helen will supervise you."

Michelina shook her head. "This is insane."

"I agree. It didn't show great planning on your part not to get insurance."

The comment stung. Michelina rebelled at the idea that she couldn't take care of herself. She might not be acquainted with everyday matters, but she could learn. She lifted her chin. "What if I refuse?"

"Then you can go thumb a ride," he said, cocking his head toward the front door. "Your truck isn't drivable."

Fighting the suffocating sense that she was trapped, she searched for another solution and couldn't think of one.

"You don't have much of a choice," he said, his gaze holding a mix of emotions as he let out a long sigh. "Neither do I."

Michelina closed her eyes for a second in search of peace and sanity then opened them again to the man currently responsible for her insanity. She swallowed her pride. "How long?"

He shook his head in disgust and headed for the door. "As long as I need you. I'm going to check the stock. Make sure the girls get dinner and baths."

Michelina stood gaping after him long after she'd watched his fabulous backside leave the house. She was trying to come to terms with what had just taken place. She had somehow become employed—however, she wouldn't have any money to show for it. And she was, of all things, a nanny!

The realization began to set in. She could envision

her brothers howling with laughter at her circumstances. Her mother wouldn't be at all amused, she thought, shuddering at the image of her cold, disapproving response. Had Michelina really screwed things up already?

The answer to that question mocked her like her worst nightmare. A tug on her jeans distracted her from her distress. She looked down to see Katie and Lindsey, their precious faces beseeching hers. Her heart softened. They really were sweet little girls— active and demanding, but sweet. She felt touched that they had sought her out.

''Lindsey's diaper is dirty,'' Katie announced.

A sound awakened Jared at 2:00 a.m. Lifting his head from his pillow, he listened as he heard the sound of the stairs creaking. He hoped Helen wasn't trying to navigate them. Or one of the kids. Waiting, he heard more sounds. He was bone tired, but knew he wouldn't sleep unless he made sure the girls were in bed where they were supposed to be. Groaning, he rose from his bed, pulled on his jeans and headed downstairs.

He immediately noticed the kitchen light was on. Hoping Katie wasn't trying to raid the cookie jar again, he stopped short at the sight in front of him.

Mimi, dressed in some kind of short silky robe that was falling off one of her shoulders, was sipping water from a glass. Her hair was sexy and sleep mussed, her legs endless, and she looked like trouble waiting to happen.

He cleared his throat, startling her so that she

spilled water onto the robe. The dampness plastered the robe to her skin, drawing his attention to her breasts.

"What are you—"

"I heard a noise and wondered if it was the girls," he said, lifting his gaze from her breasts and steering his mind from...well, lust. By his own choice, it had been a while for Jared.

"I'm sorry I disturbed you," Mimi said, reaching for a napkin to dab at her robe. "I was thirsty and awake."

"I would have thought you'd have been dead tired after a full day with the kids."

"I was," she admitted with a shrug, drawing his attention again to her breasts. "But I woke up. Time zone changes, I guess."

He met her gaze. "How many time zones?"

Her eyelids lowered slightly as if to shield herself from his question. "I didn't count," she said lightly and smiled. "You can go back to bed."

He nodded, sliding his hands into his pockets. "What are you going to do?"

"I think I may sit in the den. Would you mind if I turn on the television if I keep the volume low?"

She asked in a stilted voice, as if she were unaccustomed to asking permission. She was the kind of woman who oozed sensual luxury. From her silky, shiny, well-tended hair to her well-modulated speech and sometimes overly formal tone all the way down to her painted toenails, she gave the impression of culture and affluence. Exquisitely well-bred, he suspected, but down on her luck.

A sour taste filled Jared's mouth at the memory of a similar woman who had entered his life; he'd played the foolish white knight only to have her leave. He'd ridden that merry-go-round before. Mimi might be a curious thing, but he suspected he'd do well to put aside any curious urges she aroused. He shrugged. "You can watch the television, but reading is better for insomnia."

"You speak from experience."

He felt her gaze drift over him in speculation and his skin heated. Irritated, he brushed the sensation aside. "Yes. Follow me," he said, heading down the hallway. "I have a library."

He opened the door, turned on the light and waved his hand. "This is the result of four generations of book lovers."

Her eyes widened as she walked to the floor-to-ceiling shelves. "Brilliant. You have a wide range of titles," she said, running her fingers over the books with a caressing hand. The movement of her fingers made him feel itchy.

Brilliant. A British classmate with whom he'd kept in touch over the years often used the same expression. "Are you from England?"

Still absorbed by the books, she shook her head. "No, but I've spent a little time there. Hmm. French poetry. I wouldn't have expected to find that on a cattle ranch in Wyoming." She opened the book and gave him another assessing glance. "The copyright for this edition is four years ago."

"I graduated from Princeton and took my share of liberal arts classes," he said.

She lifted her eyebrows as if impressed. "I wouldn't have expected that either."

"I'm a third-generation rancher, but my family insisted on an east-coast education. They wanted me to be well-rounded."

"And are you?" she asked, with a playful challenge in her eyes that reminded him again that it had been a while since he had taken a woman to bed.

Jared wasn't biting. "I'm too busy to be well-rounded. Help yourself."

"Thank you. I will."

He left the room and headed upstairs, banishing the image of Mimi's silky legs from his eyes and her silky voice from his ears. Jared wasn't a weak man, but he was human. Fate had disclosed a not-so-funny sense of humor by dumping a sexy, sultry woman in his lap after a long period of self-imposed abstinence. He could tell Mimi had secrets she wasn't sharing, secrets he shouldn't want to know.

He shouldn't want to know exactly where she'd gotten her accent and classy manners. He shouldn't want to know what had brought her to Wyoming. He shouldn't give a damn how many men's hearts she'd undoubtedly left abandoned after she'd got what she'd wanted from them.

His blood pressure rose at the very thought as he entered his bedroom. Although he knew he was making an assumption, he figured it was a safe one based on her manslayer looks. He took a deep breath and stared at his empty bed. An image of Mimi lying there in invitation invaded his mind with the stealth of a secret agent.

Swearing under his breath, he paced the floor. She was just a woman. She wouldn't be here very long. He wouldn't let her into his heart the way he had Jennifer. It wasn't going to happen. Chagrined at how worked up he'd become, he took another deep breath and continued to rationalize both his reaction to Mimi and his determination to avoid her. When he slid between the covers and turned out the light, he had successfully banished her from his mind.

The following morning, as usual, Jared awakened before everyone else did. After a shower, he walked downstairs to grab something to eat before he headed out the door. On the way to the kitchen, he noticed that the light in the library was still on. Muttering under his breath over Mimi's lack of consideration, he pushed open the door and stopped short at the sight of her asleep in an overstuffed chair with a book on parenting propped on her chest.

An odd mix of emotions meandered through his gut. Even in sleep, she looked exotic and seductive. The book on parenting provided a stark contrast to her black velvet eyelashes, pouty lips, silky hair and skin. He had the strangest urge to grab an afghan and cover her.

Shaking his head, he reached for the book. Her eyelids fluttered. She stared at him for a long, sleep-bleary moment.

"Tell me I'm dreaming and it's not morning," she whispered.

He chuckled. "Sorry, duchess. You're not dreaming and it *is* morning."

She pushed her hair from her face and sat up. "Duchess?" she echoed.

"It's a nickname," he said, thinking it would also be a reminder to himself that she was off-limits. "You seem like a woman accustomed to the finer things."

She stared at him for a long moment, then laughed. "Oh, that's brilliant. I can't wait to tell—" She broke off suddenly.

"Can't wait to tell who?" he asked, curious.

She paused a half beat. "The girls. They love to play pretend, so they'll love knowing Uncle Jared plays the same game."

A manufactured tale, he concluded instantly. He wondered why she was so secretive. What did Mimi have to hide? "Uh-huh," he said, but didn't try to keep the doubt from his voice. He ran his thumb under the title of the book she'd been reading. "On-the-job training?"

She smiled and stood regally. "Refresher course. What is the weather supposed to be?" she asked, changing the subject.

"Hot. You might want to pull out the sprinkler, or the girls will try to get you to take them swimming in the pond."

She stiffened. "Swimming?"

"Yes. It's when you paddle and kick in the water."

She shook her head. "We're not going swimming. Where is this sprinkler? How do you operate it?"

"There's a half dozen of them in the garage. You hook one up to the hose and turn on the spigot and let the kids run through it screaming."

"Why must they scream?"

Jared wondered if she was from Mars. How could she not know what a sprinkler was? "They scream because it's fun and the water feels cold." He studied her. "Are you afraid of water?"

"Absolutely not," she said, lifting her chin. "I drink it every day."

She'd deliberately twisted his words. "I meant swimming in it."

"It's not my first choice of exercise."

"Did you almost drown?"

"Not me," she said, then seemed to catch herself. "My brother nearly drowned when he was a toddler, so my mother never allowed us to swim without strict supervision after that."

"Where are you from?" he asked.

She met his gaze and sighed. "East of here," she replied vaguely. "Please excuse me. I should shower before the girls wake up," she said formally, and walked out of the room.

Jared walked after her, feeling dangerously curious. "Don't you want the book?" he asked.

She turned around and reached for it. "Oh, yes. Thank you."

Jared held the book and her gaze. "Why are you here in Wyoming?" he asked quietly.

She looked at him for a long moment, as if she might trust him enough to reveal at least one of her secrets. Suddenly he had the outrageous urge to want to learn *all* of them. "It's a long story," she said, then pulled the book from his grasp and left him hanging—the same way he suspected she'd kept dozens of other men hanging.

Michelina chased the girls during the morning, then—out of desperation—took them outside in the afternoon. She broke a nail hooking up the sprinkler, but it was well worth it to hear the girls' laughter and delight. An added bonus was that they were both so tired they went to bed early. Michelina liked the effects from the sprinkler so much that she repeated the routine for two days. The third day, however, the weather turned cooler, so she took the girls for a long walk instead.

That night, as Michelina tucked Lindsey into bed, the little girl couldn't settle down. ''Want Tiki,'' she said.

Tiki was Lindsey's favorite stuffed animal. She dragged the oft-repaired droopy bird everywhere. Michelina, Katie and Lindsey searched the house, but couldn't find the toy anywhere.

Lindsey began to cry. Her howls wrenched at Michelina's heart. Helen was resting, Jared hadn't arrived home and Michelina had never felt so helpless.

''Mama told Lindsay that hugging Tiki would be like hugging her until she got out of the hospital.''

''Oh, moppet,'' Michelina said, stroking Lindsey's head. ''I tell you what. If you try to go to sleep, I'll stay wide-awake all night if that's what it takes to find Tiki.''

Lindsey's lower lip trembled, but she stuck her thumb in her mouth, nodded, then lowered her head to her pillow.

The two-year-old's courage grabbed Michelina's heart and twisted. She stroked Lindsey's baby-fine hair and pressed a kiss to her forehead. "You're a brave girl. Now, go to sleep, and I'll go find Tiki."

Michelina searched the house again and faced the unpleasant likelihood that Lindsey had dropped Tiki during their long walk earlier in the afternoon. Grabbing an umbrella and a flashlight, she went out into the stormy night.

By the time Jared arrived home from the county planning meeting, all he wanted was to grab a sandwich and fall into bed. Serving as interim mayor tried his patience. The latest insanity was Clara Hancock's insistence on a huge do for the county's anniversary celebration, and the other members of the committee universally agreed that his ranch was the optimal location for the party.

Jared growled. He'd been invaded and interrupted so much lately that the last thing he wanted to do was party. He growled again when he noticed several lights on. Couldn't the duchess at least turn off a few lights every now and then? No one was up when he entered the kitchen, and he wished he wasn't awake either.

His black lab, Leo, gave a sleepy tail-wagging welcome, but didn't move from his spot from beneath the table. Slapping together a sandwich, Jared sank into a chair at the table ready to take a bite, when Katie appeared in the doorway rubbing her eyes.

"Hey, sweetheart, what are you doing up?"

"Did Mimi find Tiki yet?" Katie asked.

"Tiki," he echoed, vaguely recalling Lindsey's stuffed animal. "What happened to Tiki?"

"Lindsey lost him today. Mimi said she'd look all night if that's what it took." Katie rubbed her eyes again. "I wonder if Lindsey lost Tiki during our walk."

"What walk?" Jared asked.

"We went on a long, long walk today."

Jared got an itchy feeling at the back of his neck. "Where?"

Katie shrugged. "Everywhere." She sighed and climbed onto his lap. "She's not in her bed."

Jared's itchy sensation intensified. "Mimi didn't go looking outside for Tiki, did she?"

"I dunno," Katie said. "Prolly. She said she would look all night if she needed to."

Jared stifled an oath.

"Can I have a bite?" Katie asked.

He sighed and offered his niece half his sandwich. He stuffed the other half in his mouth. After swallowing it, he rose and urged Katie toward her room. "You go back to bed. I've got something I need to do."

The thought of Mimi wandering out in the rain on the ranch made his gut knot. The woman didn't give the impression that she was any Sacajawea.

He hustled Katie into bed after quizzing her a little more about their walk, then returned downstairs and grabbed a slicker. His favorite flashlight was missing from the kitchen, which could be a good sign. If the duchess didn't have enough sense to stay out of the rain on a stormy night, at least she had had enough sense to take a light with her. He stepped out of the door, and the rain immediately slapped him in the face. Helluva night.

Three

———

The barn door burst open with such force that Michelina nearly wet her pants. Jared stood in the doorway glaring at her, his long black duster flapping in the wind while water dripped from his black hat. For a second, she fought the wild fear that he was going to pull out a six-shooter.

Michelina raised her only weapon of defense— Tiki, Lindsey's stuffed bird.

"Hasn't anyone ever told you not to go looking for stuffed animals in the middle of the night in the dark when you're not familiar with the territory?" he asked, walking toward her.

Michelina's heart pounded in her throat. "I've been taught many rules," she said, thinking most of the rules she'd learned had pertained to royal etiquette. "But I don't recall learning that particular one."

"You could have been hurt," he pointed out, his jaw tightening.

Even though she'd gotten lost, she didn't like his implication that she couldn't take care of herself. "How? I wasn't going to freeze. I was just going to get wet."

"You could have fallen and hurt yourself."

Michelina refused to confess that she had, in fact, fallen, and would have a nasty bruise on her right thigh as a souvenir. "I'm wet, but fine."

"And every once in a while, wild, hungry animals pay visits," he added meaningfully.

She hadn't thought about that, but it hadn't taken place either. "I haven't seen any wild, hungry animals," she returned. Except for you, she added silently.

He clenched his jaw again, then nodded. "Okay, well, since you didn't have any problems and you're happy as a clam, I'll let you continue to enjoy your evening in the barn while I head back to the house. Make sure you get back in time to make breakfast for the girls in the morning, duchess," he said and turned away.

Panic and indignation flooded Michelina as she gaped after him. "You may not leave me!"

He stopped dead in his tracks and looked at her as if she had sprouted an extra head. "Excuse me?"

She worked her mouth, but nothing came out. A first for her. *Bloody hell.* She cleared her throat and took a deep swallow of pride. "I—uh—I meant to say I would very much appreciate it if you would direct me back to the house." She paused for a moment and took another bitter swallow of pride. "I appear to have lost my way."

He cocked his head to one side. "Lost? Did I hear you say you got lost going out in the middle of the night in the rain?"

In her country, she could have had him fired, if not deported, for using that tone with her. Michelina was all too aware she wasn't in her country or on her turf. "Yes, would you please direct me back to the house?"

He let out a long exhalation. "Do you know it was insane for you to go looking for that bird on this kind of night?"

"I agree that it would have been much easier during daylight. But Lindsey was very upset, and the only way I could persuade her to go to sleep was to assure her that I would look for Tiki all night if necessary. I found the bird," she said, lifting her chin. "Even in the dark."

His gaze gentled a fraction. "So you did. Are you ready to go back, or was there somewhere else you wanted to go?" he asked in a dry tone.

"The only place I want to go is to the bathtub."

His gaze slid over her like a hot breeze, then returned to her face. "That can be arranged. Ready?"

She nodded. "There's just one other thing."

"What's that?"

"I owe you an umbrella." She lifted up the tangled vinyl and metal and frowned at it. "The wind blew it upside down within five minutes of my leaving the house."

He chuckled. "That's our Wyoming wind for you.

We may be landlocked, but we get gale-force winds every winter, spring, summer and fall. If you're not careful, it'll shake your foundations. There's no such thing as a Wyoming wuss.''

Stealing a glance at the tall, forceful man guiding her back to his house, Michelina realized the wind wasn't the only thing rattling her foundations....

As they drew near the house, Jared noticed that Mimi seemed to be slowing down. He put his arm at her back and urged her forward. ''Tired?''

She nodded. ''And a little cold.''

He glanced down at her. ''Your teeth are chattering.''

She gave a forced smile. ''Silly, isn't it? The temperature can't be that cold.''

''But you're soaked through, and when the sun sets here, there's a big drop in temperature.''

She nodded again. Her stoic silence bothered him. He had the strangest sense that it was so important to her that others not think her helpless that she might end up not asking for help when she needed it most.

''Are you sure you're okay?''

She nodded again silently. She stumbled and Jared caught her against him. Her slim body trembled. Swearing, he picked her up to carry her.

''This isn't necessary,'' she protested. ''I can walk. It's not that far.''

''We need to get you out of the rain,'' he said gruffly, inhaling a heady combination of rain and her perfume. ''I can move faster than you can right now.''

''It's not at all good form to brag.''

He absorbed her look of disdain at the same time she seemed to melt into him. "I wasn't bragging, just stating a fact."

"You don't have to lord it over me."

"I'm not lording it over you. We all have our strengths. I have more stamina, and you have more—" He stalled for a moment, considering what in the world to say next.

"I have more what?" she prompted.

Sex appeal in your little fingernail than most women have in their entire bodies. "Longer hair," he finally said, knowing it was an unsubstantial response.

"Hair," she echoed with a scowl.

"Exactly. What did you think I was going to say?"

"Courtesy, manners—"

"Mouthiness," he said, unable to resist.

She gaped at him as if he'd said the most impertinent thing she'd ever heard. "I think we might be tied in the area of mouthiness."

He grinned, carrying her up the steps to the porch and through the doorway.

"You can put me down now."

"Not quite yet," he said, climbing the stairs to the bathroom. He set her down on the carpet and turned the water on full-force.

"Thank you very much for your assistance, but I can handle my own bath," she said in a prissy voice.

Jared didn't know if it was the late hour or her tone, but he couldn't resist teasing her. "Are you sure you won't need some help? I wouldn't want you to fall asleep and drown in the bathtub."

Her teeth chattered because she was clearly still

cold, but her eyes sparked with heat. "If this is your attempt at a seduction," she said in a voice smoother than honey, "you need to work on your approach."

"I'm sure you're more accustomed to champagne and diamonds."

"Not really. I'm more accustomed to manners and courtesy."

"And men who obey your every whim," he added.

Her lips parted and her eyes widened as if he'd scored a direct hit. The knowledge brought him little joy, but he found himself fighting the urge to lower his mouth to hers and satisfy his curiosity about how she would taste.

"You may leave now," she said in the regal tone that stuck in his craw.

"As you wish, duchess," he said, and walked from the bathroom.

She pushed the door shut less than a millisecond after he'd stepped into the hallway. Temper, temper, he thought, but his deep-seated, overdeveloped sense of responsibility kept him waiting in the hallway just in case she suddenly fainted.

Instead of hearing her hit the floor, he heard the sound of wet garments splatting onto the linoleum. His mind provided the visual that correlated with the sound effects. She would pull off the shirt that had been plastered to her round breasts first. He heard two thuds. Tennis shoes, he suspected, followed by socks. Jeans next. He could just imagine her wiggling her very attractive bottom to get free from the wet denim. Her long legs would be bare. He wondered what kind of underwear she wore. Silky bikinis, a thong… An unwelcome shot of arousal heated his groin.

He closed his eyes, but the wicked visuals continued. He would almost swear he heard the snap of her bra as she tossed it aside and released her breasts. The nipples would be stiff from the cold. He could warm them with his mouth.

Jared bit back a groan when he heard the splash of water as she stepped into the tub. Seconds later, he heard her let out a long sensual moan that impacted on him like an intimate stroke from her hand.

Feeling himself grow harder with each passing moment, he forced himself to stay there two more steamy, torturous minutes, then told himself he'd done all he could do, with the exception of taking her to his bed and warming up both of them. Swearing under his breath, he reminded himself that she was just like his ex-fiancée, Jennifer. But he couldn't shake the notion that his ex would never have braved a storm to collect a stuffed bird for his niece. The image of Mimi naked in that bathtub would torture him the rest of the night, but the image of her standing drenched in that barn holding Tiki would disturb him even longer.

Grumbling under his breath, Jared trudged down the hall to his bedroom and stripped out of his wet clothes. *Chaos magnet, chaos magnet.* He could hear his sister's taunting voice play through his mind and scowled at the words. He supposed he could have let the duchess spend the night in the rain. If he were a different man.

But no, his sense of responsibility had been drilled

into him at such an early age that it ran through his veins like blood. He'd been a sucker for a woman in need of a white knight too many times to count. Only thing about Mimi was that she didn't appear to be trying to use her feminine wiles to get him to do her bidding. That, along with the fact that she hadn't attempted to shirk her child care duties, had him scratching his head.

Jared hung his clothes to dry on a couple of hooks in the bathroom and stepped into the shower. A quick, hot one and he would go to bed. As the spray spilled over him, he couldn't help imagining how Mimi's wet, naked body would look. Scowling when his body immediately responded to the seductive image, he couldn't bring himself to finish with a bone-jarring dose of cold water. After he toweled off and pulled on a pair of lounging pants, he decided to go downstairs and pour himself a shot of twenty-five-year-old Macallan Scotch. The liquor burned a trail of fire down his throat.

Deciding this was a two-shot night, he poured a second and carried it upstairs. As he rounded the corner, the bathroom door swung open and Mimi stepped out in a cloud of steam wearing nothing but a towel. The towel showed him very little pity, but her body showed him less.

The skimpy bit of terry cloth dipped dangerously low over her breasts, and dangerously high on her thighs. Her skin glowed, and her wet hair looked nearly black. She glanced at the shot glass in his hand. "How thoughtful. Is that for me?"

He opened his mouth to say no, but the expression

on her face did something strange to his gut. He cleared his throat. "Sure."

"Scotch?" she asked, taking the glass from his hand.

He nodded and watched her tilt back her head and empty the glass in one swallow. She squinted her eyes, then blinked. "Very nice. Macallan. Twenty-five-year-old?"

He nodded in surprise. "How'd you know? You don't strike me as the hard-liquor type."

"One of my brothers' friends educated me."

"And how did your father feel about that?"

Her gaze softened. "My father is dead."

Jared felt an instant of connected grief. "Sorry. My parents have passed on, too."

"Well, my mother is very much alive. Some might even say a little too alive. And then there are my brothers." Mimi winced. "When Nicholas learned that his friend had educated me on the finer points of hard liquor, his friend was banished from the palace." She cleared her throat. "So to speak. From the house, you know."

"It sounds as if your mother rules the roost with an iron hand."

Mimi's mouth twitched. "That's fair to say." She licked her lips. "Very nice Scotch. Thank you again," she said, handing him the shot glass. Then she glanced down at her towel as if she'd just realized her lack of covering. "I suppose I should go. Good night, Mr. Mc—"

"Call me Jared," he interjected, impatient with the

formality when she stood before him just one brief terry cloth away from nudity.

Her gaze met his, and he glimpsed a compelling combination of seduction and secrets in her silver eyes. He should keep his distance. She was chaos, and he didn't need her, but she wasn't quite the flighty, superficial, helpless and spoiled woman he'd originally pegged her as. A woman willing to brave a rainy Wyoming night for a child's missing stuffed bird had to possess some heart and will. And fire, he thought, suspecting that although Mimi couldn't cook in the kitchen worth a damn, she would be able to burn a man's resistance to cinders in the bedroom. And make him like it all the while.

"Jared," she said, rolling his name around in her mouth like a fine wine. "Good night." She turned, but not before the towel dipped, flashing him a peek of the side of her bare breast, a peek that made him itch to see more. Torturing himself, he watched her walk the rest of the way down the hallway, part of him praying she'd drop that towel and part of him beating himself up for giving in to the temptation of watching her.

The following night, Michelina successfully tired out the girls and got them to bed early. In no mood for television, she perused Jared's library for a while, but she couldn't fight the restless feeling building inside her. She had made zero progress finding her brother, and although she adored Katie and Lindsey, she couldn't take care of them indefinitely. There was also the matter of Jared.

She frowned when she thought of him. She shouldn't care what he thought of her, but for some insane reason, she did. She couldn't bear the idea that he thought she was some useless bimbo.

Scowling, she left the library and meandered through the house. On impulse, she decided to explore the basement. In the first room, she found discarded sporting equipment, a bag of golf clubs, baseball bats, balls and gloves, a football, a Ping-Pong table and pool table. She thought of Jared's broad shoulders and could see how he might enjoy athletics. Pushing open a connecting door, she was surprised to find a mini wine cellar. Inspecting a few of the labels, she was even more surprised at the selection. Nothing approaching the palace's wine cellar, but impressive.

Returning to the recreation room, she spotted a door on the other side and walked inside. It took her a moment to find the light switch, but when she did, her heart stuttered.

The walls held competition foils. She saw a shelf with protective equipment. *A fencing room.* Who would have known? A memory of her brother secretly teaching her the basics slid through her mind. She remembered the adrenaline racing through her as she tried to master his every instruction. Michelina had craved the challenge, but when her mother had learned of the lessons, she'd put an end to them.

Moving closer to the wall, Michelina carefully removed one of the foils and slid her finger along the cold steel of the blade.

"Careful."

She started at the sound of Jared's voice, then took

a calming breath and glanced at him. "I haven't held a foil in my hand in over ten years," she said, turning to look at him.

He rested his large, well-formed hands on his lean hips, drawing her attention down his body. Amazing how the way he stood reminded her of his physical power. The first time she'd seen him, she'd made the mistake of seeing the brawn and not the brains. Now, the combination of his muscular frame and intelligence made her stomach dip and sway. How odd, she thought, and pushed the strange sensations aside as she returned her gaze to his face.

He raised his eyebrows. "What in the world were you doing with a foil ten years ago?"

"Learning to fence. My brother taught me until my mother found out."

"Not ladylike enough?"

Michelina shrugged. "Probably. I loved it. Chess with muscles."

He nodded. "Yeah, my father taught me. I haven't played much since he died, but I couldn't bring myself to remodel the room."

"It's a nice surprise." She studied his face. "Are you any good?"

He stared at her for a long moment, then chuckled and rubbed his chin. "I'm probably a little rusty, but I could hold my own in a competition."

"Teach me," she said, the words popping out of her mouth impulsively.

Jared cocked his head to one side. "That sounds like an order, duchess," he said in a velvet voice.

Impatience and something darker shimmered through

her. She couldn't explain the desire she'd had for years. "I apologize. I've always wanted to learn, and when my lessons were interrupted, it frustrated the devil out of me. This seems the perfect opportunity. Would you, please?"

He paused for a long, considering moment and shrugged. "I can work in a few lessons." He grabbed protective equipment and handed it to her. "First things first, and the lessons will be dry," he said, in contrast to the charged vests used in official competitions where competitors are wired and scoring is determined electronically.

Adrenaline rushed through Michelina as she donned the equipment. "That's fine. After I learn foil, perhaps you could teach me épée."

"Let's stick to foil first. Let me see your position," he said, nodding his head in approval. "Not bad," he said and began the lesson.

Michelina concentrated intently on his every instruction. After a while, he agreed to let her play. She thrust and parried. Michelina couldn't remember feeling this alive in a long, long time…if ever. Her heart pounded like thunder in her chest, and she could hear her breath as she tried to keep up with Jared. He was better than he'd led her to believe, but that didn't stop her from going after him.

"You're doing well. Don't thrust without protecting yourself."

He provided just the right amount of encouragement and training. "You're light on your feet for such a muscular—" He touched her chest with the tip of his foil, and she sighed. "You're an excellent teacher. You make me want to beat you."

He laughed, and the sound rippled through her blood like a surprising shockwave. "I think you would want to beat anyone."

She paused. "Why do you say that?"

"Strong competitive spirit," he said. "Nothing wrong with that."

"I never thought of myself as a competitor."

"Maybe you never had a chance. It's not a bad thing. Some people consider a strong competitive spirit a great quality."

"Even in a woman?" Michelina asked, thinking of all the advice she'd received about not challenging a man's ego.

He nodded.

Curious and full of a half dozen emotions pulling her in different directions, she pushed back her mask. "Does it bother you when a woman has a strong competitive spirit?"

"No," he said, pushing back his own mask, his eyes lit from their play. "It's sexy."

Her gaze collided with his, and she felt a charge race through her. In that moment, he was the most compelling man she'd ever met in her life. His strength, mental and physical, was irresistible. Her heart pounded as a forbidden thought raced through her head. If she were in the palace, she wouldn't have more than one unchaperoned, unsupervised moment with a man. But she wasn't in the palace. She was on her own, making her own decisions.

Her heart pumped even faster. She wondered how

Jared would react if she kissed him. She wondered if she had the nerve to find out.

Wyoming isn't for wusses.

Adrenaline from the swordplay still racing through her, she held his gaze, dropped her foil, took a step toward him, then another and another, until she stood directly in front of him. She rose up on tiptoe, but he was still too tall, still just out of reach.

"Bend down," she whispered.

His eyes darkened. "Sounds like another order, duchess."

The possibility that he might reject her made her chest tighten with fear. She automatically covered it with anger. "I won't beg."

Just as she turned her head, he caught her chin with his fingers. "No need," he said and took her mouth.

Four

Michelina braced herself for a carnal kiss that would take her by storm. The inviting, sensual brush of Jared's lips over hers took her by surprise. How could his mouth feel both hard and soft? Back and forth, he moved his lips in a mesmerizing motion that knocked the slats out from under her.

Just when she thought she could take a breath, he caught her lower lip between his and sucked it gently into his mouth. He slid his tongue past her lips, and she felt the room spin.

Michelina moved closer to him, but their protective chest coverings formed a frustrating barrier. Even that couldn't hide his strength, and it was his strength that fascinated her. He wasn't the kind of man who would ask permission, but he also wasn't a man who would push himself on anyone. The combination was oh, so seductive.

She deepened the kiss, sliding her tongue over his, and she tasted hunger and restraint. She wondered what happened when he lost that restraint. Tilting her head to the side, she opened her mouth wider to allow him more access. He immediately took it.

Distantly she heard the thud of his foil as it hit the mat. She felt one of his hands tangle in her hair while the other slid to her back to draw her lower body against his. His obvious arousal sent a slick thrill through her nether regions.

She'd been so supervised her entire life, she'd never indulged in much more than a few stolen heated sessions of intense foreplay. Her virginity had always been very important to her mother. After all, a virgin princess would be able to draw a prize groom, a groom who would contribute to the betterment of Marceau. Whether the groom contributed to Michelina's happiness or not was far down the list of priorities.

Michelina had felt ambivalent about her sexual inexperience. Embarrassed, but she'd yet to meet a man who made her want to change her status. She wasn't certain she wanted to change her status now, but she bloody well wanted the protective vests out of the way.

She pulled back slightly and shrugged out of her vest.

"What...?" Jared asked, his eyes dark with passion.

She tugged on his vest. "You're not close enough."

His nostrils flared, and he ditched his vest, then dragged her back against him. "I can fix that," he muttered, and tasted her mouth again as if she were made of honey.

As she felt her temperature rise, she realized that no chaperons or bodyguards were going to break in and interrupt. The knowledge left her conflicted. She was on her own and she could do whatever she wanted.

Whatever she wanted...

Sinking against Jared, she reveled in the sensation of his hard chest against her breasts. She felt her nipples tingle with excitement and relished the sensation of being deliciously consumed. Inhaling his clean, musky scent, she wanted more. She lifted her hands and sank her fingers into his silky hair.

He rotated his pelvis against her and her head grew cloudy. Soft hair. Hard man.

She felt one of his hands curve around her rib cage and slide upward toward her breast. Her breath stopped somewhere between her lungs and throat. His kiss went on and on, and she didn't want it to stop. She felt as if she were tumbling in a glorious free fall that had no end.

His thumb moved closer to her breast in a sensual stroking movement. He barely brushed the bottom of her breast, and she bit back a moan as he pulled it back. Heat and a raw need she'd never experienced roared through her. She wanted to rip open his shirt and crawl inside. She wanted to feel his bare skin against hers.

Faster. Faster. Faster...

Heat and blood pounding in her head, she tugged at the bottom of his shirt and slid her hand over his warm flat belly. Jared groaned in approval, and she skimmed her hand up toward his chest.

Abruptly she felt his hand cover hers. He pulled away his mouth from hers and muttered an oath. His eyes blazing fire and incredulity, he gazed down at her. "What in hell are you doing?"

Arousal still kicking through a maze of internal barriers inside her, she worked her mouth, but no sound came out. "I— I—" She closed her mouth in horror and swallowed. She *never* stuttered.

"If you think playing with me is—"

She shook her head and licked her lips, still tasting him there. "I wanted to kiss you," she said, her voice sounding husky to her own ears.

He shook his head in confusion and took a step backward. "I don't know what you're used to, duchess, but if you're looking for a boy toy—"

"You're a man," she said, unable to keep the words from slipping out of her mouth.

His gaze held hers, and a wholly primitive sexual reaction inside her shook her like an earthquake. It was so strong, she had to lock her knees.

Jared swore again and slid his fingers through his hair, shaking his head. "I don't know what your education or experience is, but we were headed for a helluva lot more than kissing right here on the mat."

Apprehension, quickly followed by powerful anticipation, flooded her. In an instant, Michelina knew what she wanted. Her mind might be muddy with passion, but she understood, with crystal clarity, her own desire. "I told you I wanted you to teach me."

He stopped dead. His nostrils flared slightly. *"Fencing,"* he said emphatically.

She took a mind-clearing breath, and nothing inside her changed. Something told her nothing was going to change her mind or her will on this matter, but she would have to think about how to proceed. She'd never conducted an all-out seduction before, and she wasn't certain how Jared would feel about her lack of experience. He was, after all, a man of honor, and he was the man with whom she wanted to have an affair. An affair to give her memories after she'd married some other man in a union her mother deemed necessary for the betterment of Marceau. It occurred to her that, although she hadn't known it, Jared McNeil was part of the reason she'd come to Wyoming. Jared McNeil and her brother. But for totally different reasons.

She tried to change the tone, to ease the intensity, of their encounter. Picking up both of the foils, she prayed he wouldn't see her hands trembling. "You didn't like kissing me?" she managed in a light tone.

"I warned you not to play with me."

"Au contraire," she said. "I think you work so hard, you probably need a little play." She returned the foils to their places on the walls. "But we don't need to argue. Thank you for the lesson. Oh, by the way, I keep intending to ask you if you've ever heard of a man who lives around here named Jack Raven."

Facing the wall, she counted during his silence. One—two—three—four—five—

"As a matter of fact, I have."

Michelina's heart squeezed tight. She resisted the urge to turn around. She didn't want Jared to see her face. She might be ready to share her body, but she wasn't ready to share her secrets.

"He owns the best seafood restaurant in Wyoming. Considering we're landlocked, that might not be saying much. His restaurant's about forty-five minutes west of here."

She nodded and slowly turned.

"Why do you ask?"

She smiled and shrugged. "I love seafood."

With a mission in mind, the following morning Michelina took the girls for a walk to her wrecked vehicle.

A kind ranch hand named Gary strolled over to chat with her and the girls, and during the course of the conversation, he offered to get Michelina's truck road-worthy during his off-hours. He estimated that he might be able to get the vehicle mechanically ready within just a few days. When Michelina told him he'd made her wish come true, Gary blushed a bright red.

Excited that she might be able to visit Jack Raven's seafood restaurant in just days, Michelina zipped through the day with an extra spring in her step. That night she visited the fencing room again, but Jared didn't appear. She told herself his presence didn't matter. She could practice her technique without him.

Two days later, Gary informed her that the vehicle should be ready by the following evening, but the paint would still be a mess. Michelina brushed aside Gary's concerns about the cosmetic appearance of the truck. All she wanted was transportation.

High on Gary's news, she expended her energy in the fencing room after the girls went to sleep. She concentrated intently on positioning herself correctly and being light on her feet.

"I can tell you've been practicing," Jared said from the doorway.

She turned at the sound of his voice, her heart rate picking up. Allowing her gaze to linger on him, she was surprised at how happy she was to see him. "Thank you. I'll take that as a compliment."

He strolled to the wall and selected a foil, then picked up the protective equipment. "Are you ready for another lesson?"

"I've been ready," she said.

He shot her a quick glance, as if he were trying to determine if she'd intended her comment as a double entendre. She hadn't, but it would have been appropriate. She had decided that she wanted to take Jared as her lover. He might very well represent the only opportunity she would get to choose. Seducing him could be challenging, but she was very determined.

"I was hoping I hadn't scared you away," she said with a smile.

He dipped his head in disbelief. "You thought I would be intimidated by your technique?"

"Or lack thereof," she retorted lightly. "I have an

enormous desire to learn and I'm willing to practice, but my level of experience is pitiful. I won't deny it.''

Jared looked into her witchy silver eyes and tried, with only partial success, to read her. Her tone was playfully seductive. It seemed to him that she wasn't just talking about fencing…she was talking about sex. Of course, that could just be the way his mind was working. After those scorching kisses they'd shared a few nights ago, he'd been forced to take a cold shower.

He could have been doing paperwork tonight, but knowing Mimi was downstairs had caused an itchy sensation inside him. He'd squelched the idea of another fencing lesson as long as he could, and finally given in to the distraction. And Mimi was nothing if she wasn't a distraction, he thought as he put on his protective vest. As long as he kept her from drawing him into whatever her secret drama or scheme was, he would be okay. In the meantime, she would serve as an amusement.

''Let's see if we can improve your experience then,'' he said, pulling his mask in place. ''*En garde,* duchess.''

He was surprised at how much he enjoyed sparring with her. The woman was incredibly intent. If she was half that intent in bed, she could put a man in the hospital, he thought wryly. He bested her in another timed round, and she stomped her foot and tossed aside her face mask.

''Damn you,'' she said, her eyes spitting sparks at him. ''Surely you must get tired of beating me so easily.''

Unable to swallow a chuckle, he shook his head, telling himself not to be swayed by her combination of beauty and kick-butt spirit. "You would be furious if you knew I gave you an inch unless you'd earned it."

She scowled and lifted her chin. "You could at least be a little more gracious about your superiority."

"You're the one who keeps mentioning my superiority."

"Yes, but you keep demonstrating it," she said in a dark voice that betrayed a smile and gave him that itchy sensation again.

"I can stop," he offered.

"No," she said. "Please don't."

The honesty in her eyes hit him like a surprise jab from her foil. She was a little too easy on the eyes, too easy to like. He should go before he took her up on the offer she seemed to be making.

Ditching his protective wear, he returned his foil to the wall. "I should go. I need to return a call about the damned county anniversary celebration everyone wants to hold on my property. I don't know anything about putting on a party for that many people."

"I could help," she said.

Her offer caught him off guard. He glanced at her. "What do you mean?"

"I mean I have some experience planning parties."

More curious than he ought to be, he strolled toward her. "What kind of parties?"

She shrugged her shoulders. "Any kind. I've helped with both large and small gatherings. I've even helped oversee a few weddings."

"Your own?" he couldn't resist asking.

She blinked, then looked affronted. "No. I haven't ever been married." She paused a half beat. "Have you?"

He shook his head slowly. "I got close once."

"What happened?"

"She didn't want to live in Wyoming."

"Well, I guess I can see how it could feel a bit isolated here to someone accustomed to living in a larger city."

"True. The secret to avoiding cabin fever is to take trips."

"I'm in total agreement," she said with a big nod of her head.

"So you know what it's like to feel a little confined?"

"Little doesn't begin to describe it," she said crisply.

"Where did you serve your time?" he asked.

She frowned. "What do you mean?"

"I mean where was it that you felt so confined?"

She waved her hand in a dismissive gesture. "Oh, I think it was more the situation than the setting."

"And it was?"

She shrugged and looked away. "My home."

The little breadcrumbs of information she dropped for him only served to make him more and more curious. "Is that where you planned parties? At your home?"

"Some," she hedged. "Why do you ask?"

"You offered your services. I thought it'd be a good idea to find out your experience." His lips twitched. "It might have something to do with the experience you said you had caring for children."

She lifted her head regally. "Are you implying that I've done a poor job caring for your nieces?"

"Not at all, duchess. But Katie doesn't keep secrets real well, and she told me she had to coach you through diaper changing 101 with Lindsey."

She lifted her chin again. "Which just proves the point that I learn quickly and am quite trustworthy." She turned on her heel. "But if you'd prefer to plan your own party, I don't need to—"

"Oh, no." He shook his head and slid his thumb and forefinger around her small wrist before she could escape. "You made an offer. You can't take it back now."

She looked at him as if he were crazy. "I believe you're confused. I can do what I want."

"Well, I don't know how *you* were raised, but my father always told me that a man of integrity never welshes on his word."

She opened her mouth as if to argue, then closed her lips together. She narrowed her eyes at him for a long moment. "That's one more thing I like about you," she said quietly, surprising the hell out of him.

"I didn't know you liked anything about me, duchess."

She rolled her eyes. "Come on, you're not that dense. You know I envy and admire your strength. I also like your intelligence. And I like that you're a man who wouldn't welsh on a deal."

He told himself not to let her compliments turn his head. This was how these conniving women reeled in the men. If the damsel in distress act didn't work, they tried flattery. It wasn't going to work with him. He'd made a deal with *himself,* and he refused to welsh on that one. He wasn't going to fall for any more pampered damsels in distress. No way. No how.

"And I'm sure you know you have a very sexy body," she said in the same casual tone he would expect her to use when she discussed the weather.

Jared felt himself harden involuntarily.

"It makes a woman wonder…"

He shouldn't bite, he told himself, curious. He absolutely shouldn't bite. Curiosity won. "Wonder what?"

She gave a sexy, careless little shrug. "Wonder lots of things."

She seemed bold and shy at the same time, which confused the hell out of him. If he didn't know better, he would say she was giving him a come-on, but he knew from experience that it was always more complicated than that. Unwillingly aroused, he ground his teeth in irritation. "Well, I'll give you a little lesson about wondering. Wondering about the wrong thing can get you into trouble," he told her, and left before she could respond…and before he could give in to the overwhelming urge to scoop her in his arms, place her down on that mat and… As he climbed the stairs and strode to his office, his body and mind taunted him. *Wondering could get him into trouble, too.*

Five

"**O**kay, okay. I can't say no to my ladies," Jared conceded, ruffling Katie's and Lindsey's hair as they ate their midmorning snack. "I'll take you swimming in the lake today."

The girls screamed in delight.

Jared grinned, then shot a glance at Michelina. "You can come along, too."

Her stomach knotted and she tensed, an automatic reaction drilled into her since birth. He always seemed to be challenging her. As determined as she was to make sure he didn't dismiss her, she wasn't sure she wanted to take him up on the dare this time. "I don't have a swimsuit with me."

"No problem," he said, stealing a cracker from Katie. "We keep several for guests."

"But, uh—"

He cocked his head to one side and looked at her. "It's safe. You can use a life jacket if you like."

Katie, intuitive to a fault, turned around in her chair and stared at Michelina. "Are you 'fraid of the water?"

Michelina detested the idea of her fear poisoning the girls' enjoyment of swimming. She swallowed a knot in her throat. "I'm not very experienced."

"Uncle Jared will take care of you. He's a very good swimmer. He yells if we do anything wrong."

Michelina took a careful breath and saw her fate written on the wall. "Will everyone be wearing a life jacket today?"

He nodded. "Everyone." He clapped his hands together. "You girls go get your suits while I find one for Mimi."

The girls scrambled out of their chairs and zipped out of the room. Michelina felt Jared's gaze on her.

"I won't let anybody drown," he said in a low voice.

She felt the hum between them that never seemed to go away, but tried not to focus on it. "I'm sure you won't. It's silly for me to feel afraid."

"Well, you said there'd been a drowning accident in your family, and it sounds like your mother got a little overprotective. Kids can smell fear a mile away."

"Too true," she said, remembering how she'd felt when she'd seen her mother's hands turn white with fear any time she or her brothers had gone swimming. The old anxiety suddenly felt like an unwelcome, unnecessary weight on her shoulders. She looked at

Jared. Who would have known a Wyoming rancher would offer her so many opportunities to come into her own and finish unfinished business? "I guess I need a suit."

"Coming right up," he said, the approval in his eyes doing crazy things to her breathing. "But I'll warn you. None of them are designer."

What an understatement, she thought thirty minutes later, after she'd helped the girls into their suits, pulled on her ugly brown maillot and slathered the three of them with sunscreen. Even her brothers would have called Fashion Emergency if they'd seen her in *this* suit.

After throwing together a few sandwiches, they joined Jared in the foyer, and he pointed at the grandfather clock. "I'm getting old waiting on you females. What took you so long?"

Katie lowered her plastic sunglasses and shook her finger at him. "Mimi says us women should always use sun protection, so we don't get crinkly too early. Did you put on sunscreen?"

"No, but I'm out in the sun all the time."

"I bet you're gonna get crinkly."

Michelina bit back a laugh at Katie's blunt assessment, but couldn't miss the dark glance Jared tossed her way. "You've been warned," she said.

"Yeah, yeah. Let's get to the lake before the sun goes down," he grumbled, and opened the door.

Michelina and Jared strapped the girls into car seats, then got into his truck. He drove down the paved driveway and onto a curving dirt road. A beautiful small lake came into view, and the blue water reminded Michelina of the ocean surrounding Marceau. "It's lovely," she said.

"Full of fish," he said. "And the temperature is like bath water."

"Really?"

"Yep, we always fish after we swim," he said getting out of the truck.

Oh, goody, Michelina thought, her mind filled with images of worms, hooks and slimy fish. She stiffened her back and reminded herself this would only last a few hours and she would be a better woman because of it.

When Jared pulled off his shirt and ditched his wind pants, she forgot all about becoming a better woman. She couldn't help but stare. His body was incredibly distracting. From his broad shoulders to his bare, muscular chest, flat abdomen and well-developed thighs, he was the picture of masculine power. Thank goodness she could hide her stare behind her sunglasses, or he would tease her mercilessly. She helped put life vests on the girls and smiled at their squeals as they jumped off the dock. Sitting on the edge, she procrastinated taking her own leap as long as she could.

"Your turn," Jared called. "Come on in before we start making chicken sounds."

Scooting forward, she bit her lip and scraped her legs on the dock as she took the plunge. The ice-cold water took her breath away. Jared immediately appeared by her side, steadying her with his hands. He looked disgustingly healthy and warm. She didn't see one goose bump, and his dark hair was slicked back from his head, while his mouth lifted in a broad grin.

"See? That wasn't so bad," he said, treading water beside her.

"It's freezing!" she said. "I can't believe you deliberately put those children in this cold water."

"They're not hothouse flowers, they can take it. Tough Wyoming born and bred," he said with another light of challenge in his eyes.

"You lied."

He chuckled, and the sound rippled over her. She still wanted to pound him.

"It's all a matter of perspective. I can tell you with absolute certainty that there are no icebergs in this lake."

"Except for me," she muttered, her teeth chattering. "And to think I got splinters for this!"

Jared frowned. "What splinters?"

"From the dock when I scooted—" Michelina felt a wave of embarrassment. "Oh, never mind."

Realization crossed his face. "Oh, on your—" He wiped a hand over his mouth, trying unsuccessfully to conceal a smile. "That's a damn shame, considering you have a mighty nice—"

He stopped as Katie dog-paddled between them. "She looks mad. What did you do?" the child asked Jared.

"I didn't do anything," he protested.

"Mighty nice what?" Michelina prompted, enjoying his discomfort. After all, he'd done his share of making *her* uncomfortable.

He paused only a half beat. "Kick," he said. "She's a good kicker like you and Lindsey."

Lindsey beamed, and the foursome spent the next thirty minutes playing in the water. Michelina liked the playful man Jared became with his nieces. He teased and laughed and chased and even had the nerve to dunk her a few times. The only previous time she'd been dunked, her brothers had gleefully done the job. All her other escorts had been too intimidated by her to play with her. Michelina tried to imagine telling her mother to include playfulness on the list of requirements for her husband and shook her head.

When Lindsey's lips turned blue, they called a halt to the swim. Katie climbed out first, followed by Michelina. With Lindsey in his arms, Jared brought up the rear.

"I got a look at those splinters when you climbed the ladder," Jared said. "They'll have to come out."

She felt self-conscious, but refused to give in to it. "Are you offering to help?" she asked, throwing down the gauntlet to him for a change.

He opened his mouth in surprise.

"Nothing to say? Does that mean we have a new contender for the poultry contest?" she asked, then turned to towel-dry Katie. Minutes later, all four of them wolfed down the peanut butter and jelly sandwiches and lemonade they'd packed before they left. All the while, Michelina felt the sizzle of Jared's gaze on her. She knew no one but she herself or a licensed practitioner was going to remove the splinters from her upper thighs, but it sure had felt good taunting him about it.

Jared collected two fishing poles and a tackle box from the back of his truck. "Let's see if we can coax dinner out of this lake."

"Let me! Let me!" Katie cried, racing toward Jared. Lindsey popped her thumb in her mouth and searched for Michelina's hand.

"I think one of us might be ready for a nap," Michelina said, cocking her head toward Lindsey. "If you two want to fish, I could drive her back to the house and pick you up later."

Jared looked at her and shook his head in consternation. "In *my* truck? You're talking about driving *my* truck?"

Insulted by his reaction to her offer, she lifted her chin. "It's not that far to the house."

"Far enough," he said, shaking his head. "I'll take you and Lindsey to the house, then Katie and I will come back."

"Wanna fish," Lindsey said around her thumb.

"But you're so tired, sweetie," Michelina said, stroking the tike's almost-dry hair.

"Wanna fish," Lindsey insisted.

Michelina sighed. "Okay, maybe we can watch for a little while."

She sat down on the dock and pulled Lindsey onto her lap. Stroking the little girl's head, she watched Jared help Katie bait a hook and drop a line in the water. After a few minutes, he glanced back at them, then nodded and moved beside Michelina. "You were right. She was ready for a nap."

"I'm right about driving again, too. Gary tells me

I'll be able to drive again very soon," she couldn't resist telling him.

He arched his eyebrows. "Gary? Why would Gary say that?"

"Because he's fixing my truck after work."

Jared stared at her for a full minute. "And how are you paying him?" he asked in a low voice.

She got an uneasy sensation at his tone. "I'm paying him for parts, but he said he would do the labor free." She smiled. "He also said not to expect it to look cosmetically pretty."

He wiped his hand over his face and nodded. "You know he's hoping for more than a kiss from you."

She gaped at him. "He's been nothing but a perfect gentleman."

"Yeah, but you gotta know how you affect—" he pointed at her and shrugged "—men."

If truth were told, she really *wasn't* sure how she affected men—she knew only how her title and family position affected men. The intensity of Jared's gaze made her feel hot and just a little bit like a bad girl. Michelina rather liked the feeling. The possibility that Jared could want her without knowing anything about her title was heady. She carefully leaned toward him and whispered, "Why don't you show me?"

"Show you what?" he asked.

"Why don't you show me how I affect a man?"

He narrowed his eyes and leaned away from her. "Any man can do that."

"I didn't ask *any* man."

His eyes flickered with white-hot fire. "Duchess, you're asking for trouble."

She saw his biceps flex with the same tension she felt. Just as her rattled mind tried to produce a pithy but seductive response, Katie let out a yelp of delight.

In an instant, Jared was beside her, helping his niece reel in the fish. Lindsey jerked awake, her little eyebrows furrowing at the commotion.

"It's okay," Michelina assured her. "Katie's excited because she's catching a fish."

Lindsey's eyes rounded, and she shifted in Michelina's lap to get a better view. After Katie and Jared successfully collected the fish, the foursome returned to the house. Tired from their outing, the girls immediately went down for a nap, and after a long, hot shower, Michelina attempted to remove the splinters from the back of her thigh. She managed to pull out two, but the position was awkward, so she decided to try again that evening. Taking advantage of the girls' nap time, she sought out Gary and learned the car wouldn't be ready for at least another day.

Tamping down her impatience to move on her search for her brother, she returned to the house and learned that Jared planned to take the girls to visit their parents at the physical rehabilitation center. His sister and brother-in-law were due to be released any day, and would gradually begin taking over the care of Katie and Lindsey over the next couple of weeks.

Soon, Michelina realized, there would be no reason for her to stay. The knowledge tugged her in different directions. On the one hand, she was glad to have the freedom to try to find her brother. On the other hand, she felt oddly reluctant to leave. The latter feeling was related to Jared. He bothered her.

He bothered her by the way he seemed to challenge her at every turn, and she not only wanted to meet his challenge, she wanted to surpass it. He bothered her by underestimating her. He bothered her because she spent a lot of time wondering what kind of lover he would be.

Needing a distraction, she went downstairs and practiced fencing with the target dummy. Two hours later, disgusted with her performance, she returned her foil to the wall and marched upstairs. When she reached for the doorknob, the door opened without her touching it.

Jared appeared in the doorway. "I wondered where you were." His gaze fell over her. "You don't look happy."

Enormously glad to see him, yet annoyed at how much he affected her, she let out a sigh. "I sparred with the target dummy."

"Yeah?"

She walked past him. "The dummy won."

He snickered. "That bad, huh?"

She frowned. "I was horrible. It was as if I'd never picked up a foil in my life."

"Maybe you're trying too hard. Try taking a day off."

She nodded, thinking that if everything worked out, she could visit her brother's restaurant tomorrow night. "I may do that. Where are the girls? I'll help put them—"

"Already done. They'd had a big day and practically fell into bed," he said.

Surprise darted through her. "I didn't even hear you arrive."

His lips twitched. "Too absorbed in beating the hell out of my target dummy."

She shrugged her shoulders, too frustrated by him and the condition of her truck and everything else to argue. "Thank you for putting the girls to bed. I think I'll—"

"I'm ready," he interjected.

Something in his tone snapped her head around. She looked at him closely, and the masculine intent in his eyes made her stomach dip. "Ready for what?" she dared to ask.

He moved closer and skimmed his fingers down a strand of her hair. "Ready to show you how you affect a man...how you affect me."

His voice was smoky-sexy, and she felt a sudden shot of apprehension. She had thought it would take longer to seduce him. Actually, she had wondered if she would *ever* get him to be her lover. Her heartbeat skipped. Was *she* ready for this? She looked at Jared's tall, muscular body and the hungry look in his eyes. Was she ready for him?

She heard a little voice inside her taunting: *wuss.* She stiffened her resolve. This might be her only chance to choose a lover. Her *only* chance. She held her breath.

"Unless you've changed your mind," he said, his voice full of challenge and possibilities.

Her mouth went dry. "I haven't changed my mind."

He nodded in approval and took her hand. "Come up to my bedroom."

Her heart in her throat, she allowed him to lead her up the stairs. Her mind and pulse were racing. Had she thought of everything? Was she sure? Halfway to his room, she turned to him, "I must ask. Do you have—" She couldn't think of a delicate way to put it. "Um—"

"What?" he asked, the motion of his thumb on the inside of her wrist providing a terrible distraction.

"Contraception," she blurted out.

"Yeah. I'll take care of you. Don't worry," he said, lifting her hand and kissing the same place on her wrist that he had rubbed.

She felt light-headed from excitement, and they hadn't even entered his room. He led her the rest of the way down the hall and through his door, immediately turning on two lights.

"Shouldn't we turn out at least one of those lights?" she asked as he drew her against his chest.

"I want to see."

She didn't think it possible, but her heart pounded against her rib cage even harder. Then he lowered his mouth and kissed her, and the room began to spin. He darted his tongue just inside her lower lip as if he were licking her, eating her. She felt her breasts grow heavy. Skimming his hand to the top of her jeans, he deepened the kiss as he toyed with the buttons on her jeans.

Arousal pooled between her thighs, and she felt the achy need to touch his skin. She slid her hands beneath his shirt to his belly, and he inhaled sharply, grabbing her hand. Confused, she looked up at his face.

"May I take off your jeans?" he asked, dropping a distracting kiss on her throat.

"Yes," she murmured. Yes, he could do anything he wanted.

Returning his mouth to hers, Jared slowly pushed her jeans down. She was impatient for him to take off his shirt, but she supposed she could wait. Another few seconds. The urgency coursing through her surprised her.

He dropped to his knees and untied her shoelaces, interspersing kisses on her belly and knees as he removed her shoes and helped her out of her jeans.

When he rose to his feet, she slid her hand up under his shirt again, and he gave a groan that made her feel wet and wicked. "Ah, duchess, you're something else. I'm supposed to be the one showing you."

"That doesn't mean I can't touch you, does it?"

He groaned again. "Guess not. But it's my turn first." He stayed her hands again and gave her a French kiss that made her feel as if she was riding the world's fastest roller coaster. "I want you to lie down on my bed."

"I can do that," she said, her knees soft as she melted onto his big bed. She looked up at him, wanting to seal this moment in her memory. He was going to be her first lover, her first and the only one she got to choose. She riveted her gaze on him and stared. His hair was sexily mussed, his eyes dark with want, his lips still damp from their kisses. She could feel his hunger even though he wasn't touching her.

"I want you to do one more thing, Mimi."

She would do anything he asked her in that half velvet, half husky voice.

"Roll over on your stomach," he whispered.

Six

Curious why he would want her on her stomach, Michelina turned over and held her breath. She felt as if every nerve ending was on high alert.

"I've got the tweezers right here. This shouldn't take but a couple of minutes."

His matter-of-fact words penetrated her dazed arousal. "Tweezers!" She started to turn back over, but Jared's heavy hand on her back pinned her to the mattress.

"Be still," he ordered.

Mortified, then furious, she kicked at him. And missed. Bloody hell. The jerk had led her to believe they were going to make love, that he was so aroused he couldn't bear for her to touch him, when all he really wanted was to pluck splinters out of her thighs.

He caught her ankles in a viselike grip. "Cut it out,

duchess. If we don't get these splinters out, then you could get an infection and it would be my bad luck to find out you didn't have health insurance.''

She was so furious, she almost couldn't speak. ''Let me go! I don't want you touching me.''

''You didn't mind a minute ago,'' he reminded her in that now-infuriating velvet voice.

''That was different. Let me go!''

''I'm not letting you go until I take care of those splinters.''

''This is abuse. There has to be a law against it,'' she said, wishing she could snap her fingers and transport this scenario to Marceau. Her bodyguards would kill him, or at the very least, hurt him badly.

''Sorry, duchess, if you want out of my clutches, you're going to have to let me get your splinters.''

He had led her to believe he wanted something a lot different than her splinters just moments before, she thought darkly. She felt another hot wave of humiliation, but had the uneasy feeling that Jared would hold her in this position half the night if that was what he deemed necessary. A growl rumbled in her throat. ''I hate you for this,'' she told him.

''Fine. Hate me,'' he told her. ''Just hold still.''

He released his grip from her ankles, and Michelina stiffly dropped her legs to the bed. She counted to one thousand as Jared performed his surgery and comforted herself with countless evil punishments for him. *Put him on a rack.* Too easy. *Behead him.* Too fast. *Make him get a bikini wax.* Blood-curdling screams of pain filled her mind. The fantasy gave her enormous satisfaction.

She felt a pinch and jumped. "Ouch!"

"Done," he said, quickly stepping away from the side of the bed as if he knew she wanted to rip the skin off his bones. "That last one was deeper than the others."

She scrambled off the bed and stared at him. "Did you enjoy making a fool of me?"

He held up a hand. "I wasn't trying to make a fool of you. I just knew it was going to be tricky getting you to let me take care of those splinters."

"You didn't even consider being direct?" she asked accusingly.

"For about half a minute. If you're honest with yourself, then you'll admit you wouldn't have let me if I'd asked you outright."

Her fury bubbled inside her again like a volcano ready to erupt. "You have a lot of room to talk about honesty." So upset she could barely think straight, she snatched up her jeans and went to the door. She wanted to blast him. She wanted to punch him. The nerve of him! Getting her half-undressed on the pretext that he would make love to her.

Her chest knotted with indignation. An idea slid through her haze of anger. She took a deep breath at the outrageous scheme that played through her mind. Did she have the guts? She thought again of how he had played with her emotions, with her passion. Bloody hell, she did.

Taking a calming breath, she opened the door a sliver then stopped abruptly. With her back to him, she pulled her shirt over her head and unsnapped her bra.

"What in hell are you doing?"

"Almost done," she said, pushing her panties down her thighs and hooking them with her fingers. She turned around, fully naked, clutching her jeans, shirt and bra in one hand and her panties in the other. She watched his gaze consume her from head to toe and fought an unwelcome rush of heat.

He took a step toward her and she held up her hand. "I just wanted you to see…" she said in a voice that sounded breathy to her own ears. The combination of anger and nerves made her heart pound a mile a minute. "…what you're not getting," she finished, and tossed her panties in his direction at the same time she walked out of his door.

Jared almost went after her. He was one millionth of a centimeter away from going after her, hauling that gorgeous body into his arms and showing her how she affected him in every possible way.

That last little stunt she'd pulled had shocked the hell out of him. The vision of her naked body and the way she'd responded to his kisses earlier played nonstop through his mind. His skin was on fire, and he had an erection that wasn't going to quit anytime soon. He wondered if a man could burn to cinders from the inside out.

She had kissed him like a woman determined to give as good as she got. The touch of her hand on his stomach had had him in knots. It had been so easy to imagine her skimming that delicate hand down to where he was hard and aching for her. When she'd kissed him, he'd had a vision of her avid, wicked mouth flowing over his entire body, driving him to distraction, then satisfaction.

He'd wanted to touch her breasts, to put his mouth over the dusky tips, but he'd known he didn't have enough self-control for that. As it was, he still wanted to beat down her door and take her. She'd given him a good look at her slim, luscious body from her creamy throat, breasts that reminded him of peaches, the delicate curve of her waist and the inviting swatch of curls covering her femininity between her silky thighs.

It was just too easy, too tantalizing, to imagine plunging inside her moist, welcoming secrets. A groan started in his gut and slid out of his throat. He rubbed his face and swore. He'd had the most sexy, passionate woman raring to go, right at his fingertips, and what had he done? He'd pulled splinters out of her thighs, instead of sinking between them.

The wounded, indignant look in her eyes had made him feel guilty, and it had taken every bit of his concentration to focus on her splinters instead of her rounded bottom.

The worst part was that this was about more than her body. The woman was getting under his skin. If he hadn't cared about her, then he wouldn't give a damn about her splinters. She was still too imperious for his taste, but he had to admit he'd underestimated her. She had entirely too many secrets, and he wanted to know them all.

That was dangerous as hell, but true. She wasn't cut from the same cloth as his ex-fiancée. He was certain she'd come from a pampered background, but she'd been willing to work.

He liked her drive. He liked the way she treated the girls. Her self-deprecating sense of humor had taken him completely by surprise.

He liked the way she'd been looking at him when she'd thought he didn't see her. He saw admiration and fire in her silver eyes. He'd liked the way she'd made her desire for him crystal clear. Honest. She might be hiding a truckload of secrets, but she'd been honest about wanting him.

More honest than he had been with her.

The knowledge filled him with a bitter taste. Balling his hands into fists, he glanced down at the little strip of silk she'd tossed at him just before she'd left. He could have had her in his arms tonight, burning up his bed.

Regret twisted inside him. Even though he knew it wasn't wise, he wanted her. He wanted the fire he saw in her eyes, the passion she emanated. He'd been cold a long time.

He rubbed his thumb over her panties and groaned. Still hard, he shook his head. He'd been cold a long time, but he was burning up now. Jared had the uncomfortable feeling that he would be taking cold showers even after Mimi left his ranch.

Two nights later, Michelina waited impatiently after she had picked at her meal at Jack Raven's Seafood Restaurant. She'd asked the waiter if she could speak to the owner. The restaurant was bustling with activity, clanging dishes and silverware, Greek music playing in the background and quick-footed waiters eager to earn their tips. It was hard to believe that such a momentous occasion was about to take place. She was going to see her brother for the first time. Her stomach danced in anticipation as the seconds crawled by.

A harried-looking dark-haired man strode from the kitchen. His gaze landed on her, and he smiled and nodded. Michelina felt her heart race. Was this her brother? This man looked closer to his mid-thirties than his late twenties. As soon as she saw his eyes, she would know.

He extended his hand as he moved next to her table. "Hello. I'm Jack Raven. We're delighted you could join us this evening. Your waiter said you asked for me." He glanced at her still-full plate and frowned. "You not like your food?"

She shook her head. "Oh, it was delicious. I'm too full. I wanted the opportunity to compliment you." She craned to see his eyes, but the light was dim. Giving into her curiosity, she stood. Brown eyes. Her heart sank. This man's eyes were brown. Her brother had the trademark Dumont light eyes.

He smiled at her kindly. "You are very nice to compliment my restaurant. Please do come again. By the way, your accent…you don't sound as if you are from here."

"Neither do you," she said, trying to hide her disappointment.

He laughed, big and hearty. "Excellent point. Miss?"

"Deerman," she said. "Mimi Deerman."

"Mimi Deerman," he echoed, looking more closely into her eyes. "You have very unusual eyes. Beautiful. Please visit us again. I will make sure the chef prepares something special for you."

"Thank you," she said, appreciating his warmth and wishing the man had been her brother. She wished it had been that easy. She watched him leave and sank into her seat with a sigh. Now what? Distracted, she paid the check when it arrived, calculated the gratuity and drove back to the ranch.

When she arrived, she parked a little distance away and looked up at the large house, reluctant to go inside. Jared would probably be there with either questions or taunts. Every time she thought about the way he'd treated her just two nights ago, she felt herself grow hot with humiliation. Her thoughts and feelings grew inside her, making her feel as if she couldn't breathe. She opened the window. The events of the last few weeks bombarded her, and Michelina felt like a complete failure. She'd escaped from security just over two weeks ago with a grand vision of grand accomplishments, and what did she have to show for herself?

On the plus side, she now knew how to change a diaper and make a peanut butter and jelly sandwich, and she'd managed to keep Jared's nieces alive while they were in her care. On the minus side, she had wrecked her truck, been blackmailed into being a temporary nanny and, given the opportunity to improve her fencing, had found her own performance underwhelming. She'd failed in finding her brother. She'd even failed in seducing Jared.

The terrible fear she hid deep inside her surfaced. What if she really couldn't accomplish anything of any substance? What if she couldn't take care of herself? What if she wasn't good for anything except photo ops and wearing her tiara with style?

The questions clawed at her, making her feel raw and sore when she already felt wounded. A lump formed in her throat, and pressure built behind her eyes. Giving in to her disappointment in herself, she leaned her head and arms on the steering wheel and began to weep.

You really are useless. Princess Useless. The words reverberated through her brain, stabbing at her most tender places. This was her one opportunity to prove herself, and she was botching everything.

"Was the fish dinner that bad?"

Michelina jumped at the sound of Jared's voice so close to her. She swung her head to look at him as he leaned against the window of her truck. So strong, so confident, so insufferable. The last person in the world she wanted to see. Embarrassed, she swiped at her tears. "What are you talking about? What are you doing here?"

"Your fish dinner at Jack Raven's Seafood Restaurant? Was it that bad?"

She rolled her eyes in disgust. "It was delicious. How did you know where I went?"

"Gary told me he gave you directions. Did you accomplish what you wanted?"

Discouragement stabbing at her again, she sighed. "Not really." She glanced at him, resenting him. "What are you doing out here?"

He cocked his head to one side. "Well, duchess, I was afraid your wailing was going to wake every animal and human in a ten-mile radius."

She dropped her jaw. "Wailing," she echoed in disbelief, embarrassment and indignation battling for dominance. "I was *not* wailing!"

"Sounded like wailing to—"

Disgusted with him and herself, she shook her head and started to roll up her window. "You're impossible. You're the most insensitive—"

He put his hand on the window, stopping the upward movement. "Got you to stop crying, didn't I?" he asked, with the familiar challenging glint in his eyes.

She stared at him for a long moment.

"I managed to distract you from whatever was making you cry like you'd lost your last best friend, didn't I?" He shrugged those powerful shoulders of his, providing yet another distraction. "So I've got to be good for something."

She shot him a dark look. "Well, maybe that's part of the problem. You're good for several things," she said, poking at his muscular chest. "Too many things to count. And I'm just trying to find one or two things to be good for."

"I could name a couple," he said, his gaze brimming with sensual suggestions she wasn't foolish enough to believe.

"Oh, but of course," she said in complete disbelief.

He opened the door of the truck. "Come on out."

Her resentment toward him built at his order. "What if I don't want to?"

"Then I'll drag you out. Come on. Let's take a walk," he said, snagging her arm and tugging.

She scowled at him, but didn't feel like getting into an embarrassing debate where she would again fail. "Has it not occurred to you that I don't want to be around you?"

He slid his arm to her back and guided her toward the path. "Yep, but sometimes when you're upset, you don't always know what's best for you."

"And you do?" She stepped away. "If you say one word about the splinters—"

He lifted his hands. "I was never going to mention the splinters again. You won that one hands-down."

"Not quite," she said, remembering lying on his bed as he pulled out the splinters.

He stopped and turned to her. "Did you take cold showers and get no sleep for two nights?"

The dark intensity in his eyes took her by surprise. She opened her mouth, but it took an extra few seconds to form words. "Uh, no."

"Then I'd say you won."

She swallowed over a strange knot of emotion. "Funny, I don't feel like I won, but that's nothing new," she muttered.

He lifted his hand to her chin and lifted it so she would meet his gaze. "What are you talking about?"

"You, of all people, wouldn't understand," she said, his touch making her heart race.

"Try me," he insisted.

"I did."

His gaze falling over her like a warm breeze, he rubbed his thumb across her mouth. "Try me again."

Her heart stuttered. Another challenge.

"Tell me what you were talking about."

She took a quick breath of relief edged with disappointment. He wanted into her head, not into her body. Shrugging, she stepped back and looked away. "I just feel like a failure, useless."

"That's crazy."

"No, it's not," she said hotly. "I told you that you wouldn't understand. I bet you're good at just about everything you do. And I—" She waved her hand. "I'm not really good at much of anything except maybe planning a party every now and then and wrecking a truck."

"You've done a good job taking care of the girls. You're pretty good at fencing for a beginner."

"I'm hopeless at fencing."

He sighed and reached out his hand to pull her against him. "You've just had some rough luck lately. It happens to everyone. It's not as clear-cut for us humans as it is animals."

Both disconcerted and comforted by the solid wall of his chest, she looked at him in confusion. "Why are you talking about animals?"

"To add some perspective," he said, guiding her up the path toward the house. "Take Romeo, my prize stud bull."

"Why would I want to take him?" she asked dryly.

He chuckled. "Romeo is successful. He does one thing, but he does it so well that he makes a mint."

"I don't see what impregnating cows has to do with my situation. You basically set him up with a cow and he does his thing and—"

"Not quite," Jared said. "We do a lot of this in vitro."

She stared at him in surprise. "Oh my goodness," she murmured in dismay. "So, what do you do—give him photos of hot cows?"

Jared chuckled again. "It's a little more mechanical than that."

She instinctively covered her ears. "I don't think I want to know any more."

He drew her hands away from her ears. "The point is, he doesn't fight his purpose," Jared said, lowering his face to just inches from hers. "Don't fight *your* purpose."

Her chest tightened with anxiety, and she couldn't help hearing shades of her mother in his words. As far as Marceau was concerned, her purpose was to be pretty when the camera caught her and to marry a man who could bring wealth, political influence or commerce to the kingdom. Michelina chafed at that purpose. She always had. She wanted more, but she didn't exactly know what. Sinking into Jared's gaze, she saw something in his eyes that told her to look further and dig deeper than she had before.

"When are you gonna let me see the real you?"

Her breath hitched in her throat. "I think you got a pretty good look at me the other night."

"I mean what's going on in here," he said, skimming his fingers over her forehead.

Another challenge, and she just didn't have the fortitude for it. Nowhere, no how, no way. She felt weak, but if she was going to match wits with Jared, she needed to feel strong. Pulling back decisively, she replied, "Not tonight."

"Did anyone ever tell you that you're a damn frustrating woman?"

She could hear the dissatisfaction in his voice. It mirrored her own emotions so precisely that she had to laugh. "No one who wasn't related to me. What about you?"

He shot her an indignant look. "What do you mean?"

"I mean has anyone ever told you that you're a damn frustrating man?"

He opened his mouth, then clamped it shut and narrowed his eyes.

His response amused her. "That can only mean one thing. So many people have told you that you're damn frustrating, you can't even count all of them."

"You're pushing for trouble."

"I already pushed for trouble. I've got a headache tonight."

He flashed her a seductive grin. "Lady, I could make you forget your headache."

Seven

I could make you forget your headache.

Jared's velvet offer continued to dangle in front of Michelina like a forbidden dessert. After she'd turned him down the other night, she couldn't stop the feeling that she was waiting for the other shoe to drop. In this case, the shoe belonged to Jared. She'd done her best to seduce him and he'd embarrassed her, but now that she could have him, she wasn't certain she could successfully pull off the experienced temptress. She had the uncomfortable feeling that Jared would be able to see right through her.

She'd been instructed to skip the champagne when ordering supplies for the county celebration. Sitting in an overstuffed chair in the library with the door pulled closed, Michelina added lemonade to her mile-long list. The girls were spending the night with their parents with the understanding that they could call Jared if necessary. Restless and uncertain of what her next move should be, she tried to bury herself in party planning.

Out of the corner of her eye, she spotted the door swing open and her heart jumped. She'd avoided him ever since he'd caught her crying in the car.

"Haven't seen you in the fencing room lately." Jared leaned against the doorway and looked down at her. "Did you get bored?"

"No. I've been busy planning the county celebration."

He nodded. "Good. No champagne, right?"

"No champagne." *But I haven't ruled out caviar,* she thought, mentally adding it in a rebellious gesture.

"Since the girls are gone, I've got time to give you a fencing lesson. If you decide you're up to it, I'll be in the basement," he said and strolled away.

Up to it. Her temperature and ire immediately rose. Michelina stared after him. How did that man manage to get her going so easily? She should be able to dismiss him. She had dismissed plenty of other men. Her brothers had never seemed to have any problem enjoying then discarding women. Glancing down, she noticed she'd crumpled her list in her hand. She definitely needed some practice if she was going to pull off everything her brothers had done. Taking a breath, she smoothed out the paper and eyed the open door. She may as well take the bloody fencing lesson.

Walking down the steps, she prepared her ego for another beating. Jared was pulling the foils from the wall as she walked into the room.

"Have you thought about lifting weights?" he asked, as he handed her the chest protector and her glove.

"Why? I thought dexterity was more important in fencing."

"A little weight training will strengthen your hand so you won't tire quickly. There are some weights in the rec room, if you're interested." His gaze skimmed over her, then settled on her eyes. She felt something inside her crackle and pop.

"Let's warm up, then work on closing the line and the riposte today."

The plan suited her mood. In the past, he'd focused on defensive moves. The riposte was a swift return attack performed in one smooth motion after a parry. If she were lucky, she would spend the next hour poking the great Jared McNeil with her foil.

Forty-five minutes later, she was in the groove and she'd worked up a sweat. Every time Jared gave her an instruction, she made the adjustment almost before he said it. She read his body language and began to predict which way he would move.

"You're doing well," he said.

"Thanks. Do we have to stop?"

"Three bouts?"

She nodded, jumping up and down to keep her concentration up.

"Winner gets a round of truth or dare," he said, moving in position to salute.

Michelina automatically went through the motions of the salute. "Truth or dare?"

"Kids' game. Harmless," he said. *"En garde."*

She gave him a run for his money and even managed to win the first bout. She was so happy she was beside herself. Flushed with victory, she went at him again, but he soon put her on the defense and won. He was ahead by two touches, so she tried a move new to her. It took him by surprise, but not long enough. He recovered and took that bout, too.

He pushed back his mask and gave a low whistle. "You're getting better. Faster."

She pushed back her own mask, struggling with conflicting feelings. "You didn't let me win, did you?"

He stared at her for a long moment and started to laugh. "Throw a bout for the helpless female? Not my style, and you're not helpless."

She breathed easier. "Then I really did beat you?"

"In one match," he was quick to point out.

Exhilaration rolled through her. "Yes, but I still won."

"One bout," he repeated, then cracked a grin as he took her foil from her. "You like winning, don't you duchess?"

"Winning against you is a big deal. I don't think there's any need to stroke your enormous—" she paused deliberately "—enormous ego, but you know you're good."

"Good enough to win two out of three bouts, which means you owe me a round of Truth or Dare."

She waved her hand dismissively. "Whatever that is."

"So do you choose truth or dare?"

She felt a ripple of uneasiness at the predatory glint

in his eyes. She wasn't certain about the rules of this game, but she knew she didn't want to answer his questions, and she knew he had plenty of questions about her. "Dare."

He nodded and moved closer to her. "Kiss me," he said. "For five minutes."

She gaped at him. "Five minutes?" She would melt into a puddle in the middle of the floor. "And what if I choose truth?"

He shook his head. "Once you choose, you can't go back. But I'll let you this time. Who were you looking for that you didn't find at Jack Raven's Seafood Restaurant?"

Talk about choosing between the devil and the deep blue sea. She couldn't welsh, though. He probably expected that, and even though she couldn't kiss him and didn't want to reveal anything about her family to him, she was going to have to do something. She looked at his mouth. Her heart squeezed dangerously tight in her chest. Definitely not kissing.

Taking a deep breath, she told herself that she wouldn't be here long enough for Jared to cause any real damage. "My brother. I was looking for my brother."

He stood stock-still. She read the quick shock in his dark blue eyes, then she could practically see the vapor trail from how fast his mind was moving. "Which brother? How many brothers do you have?"

"Five, but I've never met one of them."

He moved closer to her, and every step closer he took made her feel more on edge one second, more relieved the next. "Does this have something to do with the one that almost drowned?"

She nodded. "Were you good with puzzles when you were a child?"

He shrugged. "Good enough."

An understatement, she suspected. Was there anything he couldn't do well?

"What's the rest of the story?"

"He was just a toddler at the time. My family was vacationing in Bermuda, and my father and one of his brothers took some of the kids sailing one afternoon. A terrible storm came up quickly, and Ja—" She corrected herself. He wasn't known as Jacques Dumont anymore. "Jack fell overboard. My uncle and father nearly drowned trying to find him, but it was as if he'd disappeared. There were search parties, but he was never found. We thought he was dead," she said. "Until last year when we received a lost letter with a lock of his hair and a button from the jacket he wore the day of the accident."

"That's why you're here in Wyoming," he said.

"Most of the reason," she admitted.

"I'm surprised your family let you take off on this search by yourself."

"I'm of age, even though they might forget that fact," she said stiffly. "Even though they may not think I can be trusted with the truth—"

Jared held up his hands. "Whoa. Whoa, there. What are you talking about?"

"It's the only-sister-youngest-child syndrome. They think I can't do anything, which is understandable because I can't do much," she said, hating the way her voice trembled. "I don't know why I'm telling you all this, because you probably agree with them and—"

"Hey," he said, giving her shoulders a gentle shake. "Don't talk about yourself that way. You haven't had much of a chance to prove yourself, but you're doing it now. I already told you that you've done a good job with the girls. And you just beat me in a fencing bout." He shook his head. "Don't put yourself down, and don't let anyone else do it either."

She felt as thought she'd just been struck by lightning. Stunned at the way he'd defended her, she stared at him, speechless. Countless bodyguards had defended her because of her title, but she couldn't remember ever feeling as if someone had defended her for herself. The strength in Jared's eyes called to something deep inside her. She felt stronger—she felt as if she were capable of anything. She felt everything but useless.

Jared slid one of his hands though her hair, tangling his fingers around it. His gaze lowered to her lips, and his mouth followed, taking hers. Desire and something deeper and more powerful crackled through her. She lifted her hands to his head, reveling in the texture of his hair in her fingers, urging his mouth against hers.

The passion between them burst like a fiery explosion, burning away reason, logic and fear. Michelina only knew she wanted to be as close to Jared as she could get. She wanted to feel the beat of his heart against her palm. She tugged at his protective chest covering, and he accurately read her silent request.

He pulled off his chest covering and hers, stealing kisses all the while.

She immediately pulled loose his shirt and slid her hands up to his chest.

Jared closed his eyes and let out a hissing sigh, then he opened his eyes, and the expression in them made her heart thud in anticipation. "I'm not stopping you this time," he said. "Even if it kills me."

A ripple of excitement coursed through her, and she slipped her palm up farther, to where his heart pounded. He took her mouth again in a scorching French kiss while she allowed herself to explore freely the muscular contours of his chest and belly.

He took her with deep, drugging kisses that left her mind muddy and aware only of him. The room faded from her consciousness. With his mouth still fastened to hers, she was dimly conscious of him undoing the buttons of her shirt. She held her breath and felt her bra loosen. She inhaled just one breath and found herself standing before him half-naked.

"I've wanted to do this too long," he muttered. He lowered his wet, open mouth down her throat to her chest, then he lifted her slightly and closed his lips around one of her nipples.

Heat flashed through her, and she felt her knees dip.

Jared caught her against him and placed her down on the floor. Following her down, he kissed her again and she arched against him, craving the sensation of his hard chest abrading her tender nipples.

"Too hot," he muttered against her mouth. "Damn, you've got me too hot."

Michelina felt herself grow swollen and restless. She wriggled against him, squeezing his biceps, sliding her fingers over him, reveling in the texture of his skin. Skimming her hands down his broad back, she encountered his jeans and frowned. "Why are you still dressed?" Stretching her arms, she slid her hands beneath the waistband of his pants to his bottom.

He swore under his breath. "You're not helping me slow down."

"I didn't know that was my purpose," she whispered, the edginess in her voice kicking her arousal up another notch.

Growling, he pulled back and ditched his jeans. Before she could blink, he had removed his briefs.

Michelina stared, transfixed by the sight of his potent masculinity. At first glance, his size intimidated her. She swallowed over a lump of emotion that mixed apprehension and excitement. That could hurt, she thought, and forced herself to take a deep breath. But she wanted this, she told herself. She couldn't let him know how inexperienced she was. Her worst fear was that he would stop.

She lifted her hands. "You're too far away."

He groaned, allowing her to pull him partially onto her as he rested on his elbows. She loved the weight of him, luxuriated in the sensation of being surrounded by him. It didn't last nearly long enough, though, before he moved his mouth down to her breasts, teasing the already tight tips into oversensitive buds. His wicked, attentive mouth tightened a coil inside her, and she felt herself stretching, reaching for more.

Reading her body like a book, he continued moving his mouth down her belly, creating sensual havoc inside her. He removed her jeans and she held her breath when he moved lower still, kissing the inside of her thigh. Then he pressed his mouth against the secret part of her that clamored with need.

He rubbed his tongue over her with mind-blowing repetition. She couldn't breathe, couldn't think. She rode the edge of pleasure and uneasiness at the carnal intimacy with which he took her. But he touched her body as if he'd known her pleasure points the moment he'd seen her. He knew what he was doing. She reacted purely out of instinct.

His tongue stroked her, and she shuddered. He groaned in approval. "You taste so good, feel so good in my mouth."

Desire and need bubbled from her body, sliding out of her throat. She couldn't stop the sounds. The tension inside tightened unbearably, and she arched against his wicked, wonderful mouth, seeking, needing, desperate. He drew the wellspring of her femininity into his mouth, and a spasm of pure pleasure rocked her. Michelina gasped at the strength of the sensations that ricocheted through her.

When she caught her breath, she met Jared's gaze. It was so hot, she felt as if she were burning alive. He pulled a foil packet from his discarded jeans, ripped it open and rolled the condom over his engorged masculinity. Wanting the rest of him, wanting to take him as he'd taken her, she leaned up to reach for him, but he shook his head and slid his thigh between hers. For a second, she noticed the rough texture of his thigh against hers, but then he was pressing against the opening to her innermost recesses. In one sure stroke, he thrust inside her.

The too-stretched burning sensation took her by surprise and she flinched, holding her breath.

He looked into her eyes, gazing at her in disbelief. "You're not—you couldn't be—"

He started to pull away, and panic sliced through her. She locked her legs around his buttocks. "You're not really planning to back out on me a second time, are you?"

"Are you a virgin?"

She couldn't resist the urge to squirm under his hard gaze.

He swore under his breath. "Stop moving."

"Stop looking at me as though you don't approve."

"Oh, I approve, all right. I approve so much, I could explode with approval. But you still haven't answered my question."

"I think I'm probably not," she said, thinking it wasn't very nice of him to embarrass her this first time.

"You *think?*" he asked incredulously. "I *think* that's something you ought to know."

"Okay, well, I'm certain I'm not now."

He hesitated a half beat. "What about five minutes ago?"

Michelina sighed. "I always heard this was a lot of fun, but now I'm starting to wonder."

"Five minutes ago?" he prompted, undeterred by her impatience.

"This isn't very flattering. First you made me strip and led me to believe you were going to make love to me, and then you pulled out my splinters instead. Now, you're grilling me—"

"If you would answer the question."

"Do you promise not to stop?"

He stared at her in disbelief, then shook his head and gave a rough chuckle. "I promise."

"I was extremely inexperienced five minutes ago."

"How inexperienced?"

"Not at all experienced. Now could we get on with this?" she asked, hot with self-conciousness. "Or maybe we'd better just forget—"

Still connected to her, he lowered himself to his elbows, his face inches from hers. "Why didn't you tell me? I could have made it better for you."

"You weren't doing half-bad until you started asking questions," she retorted, and shifted as her body began to adjust to his.

He closed his eyes as if in agony. "Are you trying to make me completely lose control?"

Seeing the raw desire in his eyes sent a ripple of arousal and feminine satisfaction through her. "Fair is fair. *You* made *me* lose control, didn't you?" she said, undulating beneath him, liking the idea of making him lose control.

He fastened his hands over her hips like a vise and shook his head. "Not this time. Not your first time."

She made a futile effort to move. "This isn't turning out to be as much fun as I thought—" She broke off when he slid one of his hands between them and found the fountainhead of her femininity with unerring precision. "Ohhhh."

Rubbing his thumb against her, causing a riot of sensations, he slowly began to move. The combination of his hand on her most sensitive place and his masculinity pumping inside her was exquisite.

"Oh, that is soooo—" Michelina instinctively arched, and Jared groaned. He continued to pump and fondle her until she felt hot and restless.

"Having fun yet?" he taunted, touching her, filling her.

"It's—" He filled her again, and the sensation made her forget what she'd wanted to say. *Fun* was such a lame word for all she was feeling. Warm, intoxicated, safe, excited. She tasted the heady flavor of a freedom she'd never experienced. The air between them grew hot and steamy and the room seemed to fade away. She was filled with Jared, enjoying the ripple of his muscles as he leaned against his elbows and thrust slowly in and out of her. She was so hot she was perspiring, so bothered she didn't know if she could bear another minute.

She wiggled, reaching for what she needed. "I want—"

His eyes heavy-lidded with passion, he strained. "You're not the only one who wants," he muttered, and the rhythm between his body and hers increased, taking her breath away.

Faster, faster, she felt the earth slide away from her as her body rocked into orbit. She felt Jared stiffen in release and clung to him with all her strength. He dipped his head against her shoulder. Their passion-heavy breaths mingled with each other, and Michelina reveled in Jared's chest against her breasts, his hard belly against hers and the sensation of his thighs rubbing the inside of hers. She had never felt so close to another person in her life.

He lifted his head and looked into her eyes, his gaze simmering with emotion. The combination of erotic possessiveness, sensual satisfaction and something deeper, more tender, made her heart feel tight and achy. "You okay?" he asked, lifting his hand to stroke her cheek.

She nodded, still trying to catch her breath. "Yes, but I want to do this again."

He stopped, searching her gaze. "When?"

"Now."

He closed his eyes. "You'll be sore."

Michelina could have purred. "I've gotten sore from fencing, and I like this a lot more than I like fencing."

Eight

It had been a long time since Jared had shared his bed with a woman like Mimi. He thought of his ex-fiancée and mentally shook his head. He'd never *had* a woman like Mimi in his bed. The woman hummed with secrets. That was why he was staring at her at 5:00 a.m. after they'd spent the night burning up his bed.

Jared had covered every inch of her very fine body, but he still had questions. Her body told him stories. Her body told him what she liked. She liked a firm, sure touch. She liked to be teased, but only for a while. She liked long kisses that left her breathless and made him so hard he ached. She might have been a virgin, but she was a fast learner, and if he wasn't careful, she would be the death of him.

Her gaze and touch told him she liked his body and

she trusted him. Partly trusted him, he corrected. He could still feel her secrets brewing under her silky-soft skin. When she'd told him she was looking for her long-lost brother, she might as well have sent a laser through his wall of protection against her. When she'd told him she knew he didn't believe she was capable of much of anything, he'd known he would have to prove her wrong. He'd never seen anyone who needed someone to believe in her more than Mimi.

He knew she was from a wealthy, pampered background. She'd been sheltered so much, she felt lost in the real world. Given the protective family, he wondered if her lack of a practical education had been calculated. If she didn't know how to get into trouble, then she couldn't cause a lot of trouble. Yet it looked as if she was making up for lost time now.

But she wouldn't stay around here long.

He heard the internal warning loud and clear and planned to heed it. Just because he'd let Mimi into his bed didn't mean he had to let her into his heart. Sure, she'd brought light and fire into his home, and he would enjoy her for the moment. Without getting too involved, he might try to help her find her brother, and he wouldn't turn down the offer of her body.

When she left, she would keep her heart and he would keep his and they would both have nice memories. It was best that way.

The sun peeked through the curtain opening and the room glowed with the gentle light of dawn. Inhaling the floral scent of her hair, he glanced down at her and felt his gut twist. Her features were soft in slumber, and that busy mouth of hers was still, but swollen from kisses. She lay on her side, the sheet covering the tops of her breasts like a strapless white gown. She was the kind of woman a man wanted to dance with in the moonlight. He lifted a stray strand of midnight-colored hair from her forehead, and she shifted. Her movement sent the sheet south, revealing her dusky-pink nipples. Jared remembered how her breasts had felt in his hands, in his mouth. He remembered how responsive she had been.

He felt himself grow hard. Unwilling to wake her, but reluctant to leave her spell just yet, he moved next to her, positioning his chest against her back while he slid his hand around her waist. She nestled her bottom against his crotch, and Jared became reacquainted with the true meaning of torture.

He stayed stock-still, but he was hyperaware of every breath she took. Her bare bottom wiggled again, and Jared swallowed a groan. Maybe this hadn't been such a good idea after all. He felt her yawn and wondered if she was waking up. She slid her hand down over his and sighed, wiggling against his swollen erection again.

"You are the most wiggling woman I've ever met," he muttered.

"Good morning to you, too," she said in a sexy, sleep-husky voice. "Are you complaining?"

"Yes and no," he said darkly.

"Why yes and no?"

He sighed. "Yes, because it's torture every time you move against—"

"Against what?" she asked, wiggling as she turned

slightly. "Oh," she said, realization seeping into her tone.

"No, because there are some advantages to this position and your tendency to wiggle," he said, sliding his hand upward to her breasts.

"What kind of advantages?"

He found her nipple and toyed with it until it grew stiff. Mimi wiggled again. Jared pressed his face into the nape of her neck, inhaling her scent, letting himself sink into a well of desire. "Do you want me to *tell* you or *show* you?"

"Both," she said. "I like the sound of your voice."

"Okay," he obliged, although he found it hard to talk while being distracted by her incredible body. "One of the advantages is that I have a lot of freedom with my hand. I can touch your breasts and play with your nipples." He stretched his hand to cover both of her breasts and reveled in the way she arched against his palm. Once again, her body told him what she wanted. He rolled one of her nipples between his thumb and forefinger, and she moaned in pleasure.

"Good?"

"Yes, but—"

He knew what she wanted, and he damn well was going to give it to her. Sliding his hand down her belly and lower, between her legs, he searched and found her wet and waiting for him.

"Like that?" he asked, feeling her tiny, sensitive bud bloom under his caress.

"Oh, yesss." Her voice was practically a purr.

He dipped his finger inside her while he continued

to move his thumb against her hot spot. He felt her skin heat, and her breath came in shallow little sexy gasps. She slid her legs farther apart, and the invitation nearly sent him over the edge. The way she trusted him with her body was irresistible.

He felt his own skin heat up and had trouble breathing evenly. She made a soft, sultry keening sound, and her body arched in complete pleasure.

''Oh, you—that—oh—'' She stopped and gasped as if she couldn't find the words. ''That was wonderful, but I wanted you inside—''

Unable to deprive himself any longer, Jared shifted her derriere and slid inside her tight, wet feminine core.

She made a surprised sound and went still.

''Okay?'' He hoped so, because he was about to explode.

She wiggled. He groaned.

''I didn't know,'' she said, wiggling again. ''I didn't know you could do it this way. The only thing is that I want to kiss you.''

''Hold that thought,'' he said, and began to pump inside her.

He thrust and she wiggled, and it didn't take much for her to fall apart again while he went spinning straight through the roof.

Over the next few days, Lindsey and Katie came to Jared's house less and less frequently. Michelina tried to occupy herself with plans for the party, but she missed the busy activity Jared's nieces had provided. What truly distressed her, however, was how much she missed Jared when he was gone during the day.

Rolling her eyes in disgust at herself, she stomped down to the fencing room and took up her foil against the target dummy. With her concentration in the toilet, she wasn't performing much better than the last time she'd faced off with the target dummy.

The disappointed, disapproving faces of her mother and brothers flashed through her mind over and over. She felt the poison of failure seep through her veins. She hadn't located Jacques. Her family wouldn't view her ability to change a diaper as particularly impressive, and there would be bloody hell to pay when they learned she'd managed to lose her virginity. And they would find out. As a royal, she had to let her body be dissected and inspected on a regular basis.

The prospect of returning to Marceau turned her stomach. Her mother would be furious. Her brothers would disapprove. She didn't want to go back, but she didn't have any idea where her long-lost brother was, and the money she'd brought with her wasn't going to last forever.

Being with Jared made her feel safe, wanted, almost normal. The physical intimacy they shared made her want to tell Jared everything, but she was scared spitless he would reject her if he knew who she really was. And the longer her deception continued, the more trapped she felt. She rammed her foil into the dummy in frustration.

"The goal is to tap her, not gut her like a fish," Jared said from behind her.

Michelina jumped at the sound of his voice. "Oh!

I didn't know you were there." She shook her head in confusion. "Did you say 'her'?"

"Jennifer," he said, his face turning dark with displeasure.

She raised her eyebrows. "What a pretty name for such an ugly dummy."

He grunted, shrugging his shoulders as he walked toward her.

"Does she have a human namesake?"

"Yes. My ex-fiancée. She came running to me when she got embroiled in a scandal that involved finances, then married her attorney instead."

Michelina blinked and glanced again at the target dummy. "I see the resemblance," she said, her lips twitching.

"How can you see the resemblance? You've never met the woman."

"I meant the resemblance in terms of intelligence. For her to leave you for an attorney, she had to be quite stupid."

He stared at her for a long moment, during which she saw a dozen emotions come and go in his eyes. "How do you know the attorney wasn't the better man?"

"Because I know you. And I haven't met a better man," she said, the truth of it hitting her fast and hard.

"Maybe you haven't met a lot of men," he ventured.

"I've met dozens. No, make that hundreds."

"Hundreds?" he asked, arching his eyebrow in disbelief.

"Hundreds," she said firmly. *If not thousands.* She thought of how many men's hands she'd shaken, how many she had joined in a dance, how many she had entertained at dinners and formal events.

"Why were you so intent on destroying Jennifer?"

She shrugged. "Just working off some of my frustration."

"What's got you frustrated?" he asked, lifting his hand to chuck her chin.

His closeness muddled her mind. She looked away so she could think straight. "I've been thinking about my brother."

"Which one?"

"All of them," she reluctantly revealed. "But mostly Ja—" She cleared her throat to cover the French pronunciation of Jacques. "Jack." She pulled off her glove. "This is going to sound silly, but now that the girls are gone, the house feels terribly empty."

He chuckled. "Don't tell me you've got too much time on your hands. The county celebration is in just a few days."

She waved her hand in a dismissive gesture. "I've got all that covered."

"The library could use some help."

Her curiosity immediately piqued, she looked up at him. "What kind of help?"

"A lot of the books are falling apart in the county library and we haven't had anyone step up to boost the inventory."

"What about that Clara person you mentioned?

The one who insisted on holding the county celebration on your property?''

Jared shook his head. ''She runs the volunteer station at the hospital.''

''But this would be so easy. All it would take is a book drive. Ask people to donate the cost of a book and insert a bookplate with their name in recognition of their donation. For that matter, you could set up a table at the county celebration and jump-start the donations then.''

''So when are you going to get started?'' he asked.

Michelina gave a double take at the challenge she heard in his voice. ''I would need some assistance, some names.''

''I could help you out with that.''

''I can't make a long-term commitment,'' she told him, and she was talking about more than the book fair. She couldn't stay here in Wyoming with Jared indefinitely. She kept reminding herself that she was going to have to face her responsibilities, lame though they seemed, in Marceau sometime. Her stomach clenched. Most likely sometime soon.

His gaze grew hooded and unreadable. ''No one is expecting you to make a long-term commitment, duchess,'' he said in a too-smooth voice that chilled her.

Her heart clenched at his remote air. ''I wasn't saying that I'm incapable of making a long-term commitment. It's just that I know I'll have to return—''

''Where?'' he asked with an edge in his voice.

''Home,'' she said, nervous at the intensity humming from him. She didn't want him asking too many questions, because she still wasn't ready to answer them. "If you can supply me with some names of people willing to help, I'll organize the book drive."

"Good," he said, and took the foil from her hand. He hung it on the wall and turned back to her. "You should have told me you felt frustrated, Mimi. I could have helped you with that."

Even though they had made love several times, the dark sexual expression in his eyes made her heart race with jittery excitement. She laughed, trying to lighten the atmosphere, which was thickly layered with opposing emotions. "Are you saying you could have helped increase my frustration? I think you've already done that," she joked.

"Me?" he asked, his innocent tone belying the way he backed her against the wall. "I'm just a simple Wyoming rancher. How could I frustrate a duchess?"

"Simple," she scoffed, trying to keep a clear head even as Jared lowered his mouth toward hers. "You and Romeo have a lot in common. You're both full of bull."

"You're entirely too mouthy, but shutting you up is a helluva lot of fun for both of us," he said, then took her mouth in a hot French kiss that made the room spin. She tasted passion and a mirrored frustration in his kiss, and felt the desire to absorb as much of him as she could in the short time she was allowed. The more she learned about Jared, the more certain she grew that she would never meet another man like him. The uneasy suspicion that she would never feel this way about another man jabbed at tender places inside her with the precision of an accomplished fencer.

Michelina closed her mind to everything but him. She couldn't think about tomorrow. Tomorrow would be slapping her in the face soon enough. Just for now, she could be safe and wanted in Jared's arms. Just for now, she could trust that he wanted her for her. And that had to be enough. She tugged at his belt, eager to get closer.

He groaned and stilled her hand. "When am I going to get enough of you?" he muttered, then swung her over his shoulder.

Michelina yelped. "What are you doing?"

"Doing my duty and hauling you off to my bed to take care of your frustration," he said dryly, striding out of the fencing room and climbing the stairs. With each step, his shoulder jabbed her abdomen.

"Duty?" she echoed, frowning, not liking the use of that term. "Duty is changing a diaper."

"It's a matter of opinion," he said mildly, as he allowed her to slide down his body.

He kissed her again, and although she could feel the evidence of his hard desire against her thigh, she was still bothered that he'd even uttered the word *duty*. She'd come from a world of duty, and that was where she would return. Her stomach turned. She pulled her mouth from his. "I never want you to do *anything* for me out of a sense of duty."

He studied her for a long moment. "What if I consider it my duty as your lover to take care of your frustration?"

The combination of seduction and tenderness in his eyes knocked the breath and the fight right out of her.

His lips lifted in a lazy half grin. "What? Is this a first? Duchess has nothing to say?" He rubbed his thumb over her bottom lip. "There you go, underestimating yourself again."

A lump of emotion formed in her throat. She swallowed over it. "How?"

"I'm gonna show instead of tell this time," he said, sliding his hands beneath her shirt and lifting it over her head. "But before I go any further, there's one question I want you to answer."

He turned toward his bureau, and she spotted her tiara as he picked it up. Michelina's heart stopped. Panic froze her blood in her veins.

Extending his hand, he waved the tiara in front of her. "Leo brought this to me when I came in this evening. It doesn't go with any of my attire." His gaze pinned her with the force of a nuclear missile. "You want to tell me what you're doing with it?"

Nine

Michelina felt as if her brain had locked up and someone had thrown away the key. "Um, it's a, uh…"

"Yes?" he prompted, clearly expecting an explanation.

"Um, it's an accessory," she said. "Like a hat."

"A hat," he echoed skeptically.

"Yes, it's an accessory women wear…to parties." She forced her lips upward in a smile, trying to keep the terror she was feeling from her face.

"Parties," he said, and shook his head. "I have to tell you, I haven't seen any women wear one of these to any barbecues I've attended."

Michelina had no answer to that.

"I've only seen women wear tiaras for three different reasons. One, if she's royalty."

Michelina held her breath.

"You get a funny accent in your voice every now and then, and you like to give orders, but if you were really royalty, I don't think you would have lasted an entire day with my nieces, so that's out." His gaze turned cool. "The second reason a woman might wear this thing is if she's a bride."

Michelina glanced at the tiara and shook her head. This was her ready-to-wear tiara. Her bridal tiara would be far more elaborate. "I've never been a bride."

"That leaves the third possible reason." He sighed, rubbing his thumb over the pearls and diamonds. "Beauty queens wear tiaras."

He looked at her expectantly, and Michelina gave him a blank stare for a full moment before it hit her. He thought *she* was a beauty queen. *Omigoodness.* The urge to laugh hysterically backed up in her throat. She felt her eyes burn with tears with the effort it took to swallow her laughter. "I don't know what to say."

"Don't deny it," he said.

Her stomach twisted. She didn't want to lie to him. "I can't deny that I've been trying to escape the image some people have of me."

"Beautiful, but that's about it," he said.

"Exactly."

He put the tiara on the bed, then turned to her and pulled her into his arms. "You're beautiful, but you and I both know there's a lot more to you than the way you look."

What he said and the way he looked at her made

her feel wonderful and horrible. No one had ever ver-
balized such belief in her, and right to her face. The
power of it rocked through her. Seeing the conviction
in Jared's eyes made her feel as if she could do anything, be anybody she wanted to be.

Feeling his belief in her also made her feel like a
slug. He deserved the truth about her. She bit her
tongue to keep from confessing. She couldn't help
believing that once he knew who she really was, he
would look at her differently, and she couldn't bear
the prospect of that.

He had no idea how desperately she needed what
he offered her. With all her family's wealth and position, this was what she had craved her entire life.
"Thank you," she said, fighting a sudden urge to cry.

"For what?"

"Just thank you," she said, and stood on tiptoe to
press her lips to his. Later, when he learned her real
name and was angry with her deception, she prayed
he would remember this moment. She knew she always would.

Just a few days later, Jared was preparing for the
onslaught of the county celebration. Mimi was checking off items on her to-do list with a calm efficiency
that impressed the hell out of him. He suspected most
women would have been nervous at the prospect of
entertaining three hundred people, but Mimi was un-
fazed.

He'd been dreading the bill, but she had managed
to get businesses and individuals to donate almost all
the necessary food and services. He'd caught her on

the phone one afternoon asking a local grocer to donate lemonade, and by the end of the conversation,
he could tell she'd had the guy ready to hand over
the keys to his store. She'd insisted that the owner
post a sign bearing the grocery-store name at the
county celebration.

Mimi was very big on giving credit to everyone
but herself. On the day of the celebration, Jared noticed she kept giving the reporter from the county
newspaper the slip. After one close call, Jared caught
her nearly hyperventilating behind the barn.

"Maybe I should have allowed you to serve champagne," he said. "Roger's harmless."

She shook her head. "He's armed and dangerous—
he has a camera. You're mayor. Can't you expel
him?"

Jared chuckled. "No way. This is one of very few
big local events."

"I beg you to break his camera."

Jared would have chuckled again at her ridiculous
request, but he could tell she was dead serious. "The
circulation for the weekly paper is only a couple thousand." His heart twisted at the hopelessness in her
silver eyes. "Duchess, it isn't the *New York Times.*"

She lifted her hand to her throat and took a deep
breath. "I know, but—but—" She took another
breath. "You don't understand. I just—" She shook
her head. "I'll just stay in the background, and,
please, whatever you do, don't send him my way."
She pulled away from Jared and prepared to
dash away.

He snagged her hand, shocked at the temperature of her skin. "Mimi, your hands are ice-cold."

She visibly collected herself, and he watched a transformation before his very eyes. Her hands remained cold, but she lifted her lips in a sexy smile and raised her shoulder in a coquettish gesture designed to distract. It almost worked. "Me? Cold? Then maybe after this is all over, you can help warm me up." She stood on tiptoe and brushed her lips against his. "Pardon me while I check on the book drive. *Ciao.*"

Then she flowed away from him like a fine mist. He had the odd sense that he should be protecting her. She seemed strangely vulnerable, and it was unacceptable to him to allow anything to happen to her. Everything inside him rebelled at the notion that she felt unprotected.

"Hey, Jared."

He heard the familiar voice of his brother-in-law and had to tear his attention away from Mimi.

"Jared," Bob said, still limping from the injuries he'd sustained in the automobile accident. "I know I've thanked you before, but—"

Jared lifted his hand. "Stop right there. You've thanked me enough. I was glad to help with Katie and Lindsey, and Mimi did the bulk of child care duty."

Bob smiled. "They talk about her all the time. Something about how she let them try on her princess crown. Where is she from, anyway?"

"Back east," Jared said, supplying Bob with the same vague answer Mimi had given him. It rankled him that he didn't know more. He knew every inch of her body, but not much more.

He chatted another few moments with Bob, then a neighbor rancher joined in the conversation. A council member complimented Jared on the success of the celebration and tried to persuade him to take on the job of mayor permanently. Jared immediately shook his head. Then just as he was ready to refuse unequivocally, he heard a commotion near the lake.

He quickly scanned the area and caught sight of a feminine blur wearing a pink shirt and low-slung jeans leaping off the pier, her midnight hair flying behind her as she plunged into the water.

His heart stopped, but his feet immediately moved forward in large steps. "What the—" He began to run. Why had Mimi jumped into the lake? She was afraid of the water and had entered it only very reluctantly with himself and the girls. A crowd ran down the pier, obstructing his view. Muttering "Excuse me," he elbowed his way through the throng.

He spotted Mimi clinging to the ladder with a wailing toddler in her arms and felt a surge of relief. Out of the corner of his eye, he saw Roger Johnson snapping photo after photo. Jared couldn't blame him. Great photo op. But Mimi would probably drown herself when she noticed him taking her picture.

Jared made an instinctive decision. He came up behind the local reporter, clapped his hand on his shoulder and took Roger's camera right out of his hands.

Roger gaped at him. "What are you doing? That's the best photo I've ever taken. I could win an award for that."

"Sorry. Gotta respect Mimi's modesty. That water made her shirt transparent."

"I could crop it," Roger argued.

"No."

"No?" Roger echoed, incredulous. "You're tampering with the First Amendment, Jared. You could be stripped of your title as mayor."

"Please," Jared said with all sincerity, "strip me. Do *you* want the job?"

Roger shot him a look of pure disgust. "Jared, this just isn't fair."

"I'll tell you what. I'll save the film and let Mimi decide."

The reporter made a face. "What am I supposed to use in place of that photo?"

Jared shrugged. "I don't know. Romeo's photogenic." Clutching the camera in one hand, he pushed through the crowd. "Anybody got a towel or blanket?" he asked. Someone thrust a couple of baby blankets into his hand. He tossed one to the woman collecting the toddler from Mimi.

Seeing her still clinging to the ladder in the water made his heart twist. He knelt down and extended his hand. "Here, baby. Come on." Her gaze locked with his, and she took his hand. The gesture of trust grabbed at him. As soon as he pulled Mimi up on the deck, he wrapped the baby blanket around her shoulders and urged her down the pier, away from the crowd.

"Wait! I have to thank you!" a woman's voice called out.

Jared reluctantly paused when a young woman ran

toward them with the drenched toddler on her hip. He recognized the excited mother immediately. "Mimi, this is Susan Carroll."

Susan's eyes filled with tears. "I don't know what to say. I thought my niece was watching her. I feel so horrible. Thank God you saw her on the pier!"

"They move so quickly at this age," Mimi said. "I'm glad I could help."

"Thank you so much. I don't think I could have handled it if anything had happened to her," Susan said. "I'm never letting her near water again unless I'm right with her."

"Good plan," Jared said, seeing more of the crowd come toward them. "We should get Mimi back to the house so she can get changed."

Susan nodded, and Jared led Mimi toward the house.

"Thank you," Mimi said breathlessly. "I couldn't believe it when I saw that toddler all by herself on the pier. I would have screamed, but my vocal chords seemed to freeze."

He suspected she had been slammed with the memory of her brother's drowning when she'd looked at that little girl. "You did the right thing. Susan was damn lucky you were in the right place at the right time." Mimi stumbled, and he scooped her up to carry her.

"Oh, my," she said, and wrapped her arms around his neck. "This is insane. It wasn't a big deal, but I swear my knees are weak."

"It was a big deal. That kid could have drowned.

The only problem is, you've just become the county's official heroine.''

She met his gaze in confusion, then she glanced at the camera. Looking slightly ill, she touched the strap. "Did you take this camera away from the reporter?"

He nodded.

"I couldn't let that toddler drown."

"Damn straight you couldn't. You did the right thing."

"Could we rest for a minute? I want to stop and catch my breath."

Filled with fiercely protective feelings for her, he paused beside a tree and gently squeezed her against him.

"I'm getting you all wet," Mimi said, clinging to him.

"Do you think I mind?" he asked, hearing the huskiness in his own voice.

She buried her face in his throat. "No, thank goodness."

"What do you want to do about the rest of the celebration? Do you want to stay in the house? Do you want me to get one of the ranch hands to drive you somewhere?" A half-dozen scenarios sprang to his mind.

She sighed, her breath gently tickling his skin. "Right now I don't want to think about it. I want you to kiss me."

"That I can do," he said, and took her mouth with his.

Mimi tried to keep a low profile during the rest of the county celebration, but the combination of low profile and Mimi was like oil and vinegar. Even with her hair pulled back in a low ponytail, sunglasses shading her distinctive eyes, and her wearing jeans and a fitted black T-shirt, she oozed glamour and beauty. The men were tripping over themselves to help her, and the women seemed fascinated by her sophistication. She was a walking billboard for what men wanted and what women wanted to be.

By the time everyone left and the clean-up was completed, she sank down on the sofa in the den with a promise that she would just take a short rest. An hour later, she was sleeping so deeply that Jared suspected the house could fall down around her and she wouldn't wake up.

Restless and bothered, he paced his office and took care of some ranch business. Checking the clock, he decided to give Jack Raven a call.

"How did I rate a call from the top rancher in the state?" Jack asked. "Are you getting married? Do you need a restaurant for your reception?"

Jared rolled his eyes. Jack was always drumming up business. "No chance. I need a favor. I have a friend who is looking for someone by the name of Jack Raven. Do you have any cousins with the same name?"

Jack gave a low, rumbly laugh. "Only about twenty-five. I'm Greek. Half my male cousins are Nick. The other half are Jack. What age Jack you looking for? Who is this friend?"

"My friend is female," Jared reluctantly revealed.

"Is she pregnant?"

"No. She's looking for a man in his late twenties."

"That cuts the list down to five. There's my cousin Jack in Boston. I have another cousin Jack in Roanoke, Virginia. Two in Chicago. The closest one is in Denver, but he's a loner, almost a recluse. He made a lot of money in real estate, and he doesn't come to family gatherings. He has weird-color eyes. Now Jack in Boston, he's a ladies' man and—"

"What do you mean weird-color eyes?"

Jack paused. "They're weird. Very light, almost silver-looking."

The vision of Mimi's face and her distinctive eyes slid through his mind and Jared's instincts went on high alert. "Thanks," he said to Jack. "Where exactly does Denver Jack live?"

Michelina slept in the following day and surprised herself by taking a nap in the afternoon. That evening, Jared insisted on giving her a fencing lesson. As they sparred, she felt the tension hum between them. There was always a sensual, emotional sense of expectation that made butterflies dance in her stomach. But there was also the ticking clock, reminding her that her time with Jared was growing short. She was running out of excuses to stay. She suspected Jared could feel it, too, even though neither of them mentioned it.

The tension between them was so thick, she could barely breathe. Midway through a match, he grabbed her foil and tossed it, along with his, to the side. Cradling her with gentle hands, he took her mouth in a hard claiming kiss that spiraled out of control. Soon their clothes were discarded and they were making love on the floor. He carried her up to bed, and they fell asleep in each others' arms.

Michelina awakened to discover Jared watching her. She lifted her hand to his strong jaw, wanting to memorize how his face looked in the morning. She never wanted to forget how safe yet strong she felt in his arms.

He slid his fingers down a strand of her hair. "Pack a bag. I'm taking you to Denver this afternoon."

Her stomach twisted. Was he so eager to be rid of her? "Why?" she asked cautiously.

"I got a lead on another Jack Raven."

She stared at him in surprise. "How?"

"I talked to our local restaurateur, and he mentioned a cousin by the same name who lives in Denver." He brushed his thumb over her cheek. "Sounds like he might have your eyes."

Michelina sat up. "What? What do you know about him? How old is he? He has my eyes? How do you know? How—"

Jared pressed his finger over her lips to silence her. "I don't know much, but I'll tell you about it on the way. I've got to cram a whole day's work into a few hours right now. It's a maybe, but this guy sounds like he's the right age, and I haven't seen many people with eyes the same color as yours."

Michelina's heart hammered in her chest. "Oh, Jared, if he's my brother, if he's really my brother, this will be fantastic. Amazing! Do you realize I can't remember ever seeing him? The only way I remember him is through pictures. If this is him…" Her voice broke with emotion, and she felt her eyes fill with tears. "I can't tell you how much this means to me."

"Try to keep your hopes under control," Jared cautioned her. "I don't want you to be disappointed. It's a big maybe. Remember that. Maybe." But he hoped with a fervor that took him by surprise that Mimi wouldn't be disappointed.

Ten

Jack Raven's office in Denver wasn't designed for drop-in visitors. By the time Jared and Michelina reached the penthouse suite, she wondered if Raven Enterprises had more gatekeepers than the royal family of Marceau. Thank goodness Jared had known someone who could get them past the first few barriers.

"Do you have an appointment?" the woman at the desk asked after Jared had given their names.

"No," Michelina said for the umpteenth time to the umpteenth assistant.

"We're interested in learning more about Mr. Raven's resort development in Costa Rica," Jared said smoothly.

Michelina stared at him. "We are?"

He took her hand and gently squeezed it. "Of

course we are. Remember we discussed it after we looked into land development in Arizona?''

"Oh." Michelina nodded slowly at the ruse. "We've looked at so many that I didn't remember if we were looking at Costa Rica or Mexico."

"We have excellent project managers who could help you," the assistant said.

"We prefer to see Mr. Raven," Jared said in a nonnegotiable tone.

The assistant sighed and punched a button on her phone. "Miss Dean, we have some potential investors, Mr. McNeil and Miss Deerman. They insist on seeing Mr. Raven." She nodded and listened, then turned to Michelina and Jared. "Mr. Raven's personal assistant will see you."

Michelina was so frustrated, she nearly stamped her foot. "But—''

Jared squeezed her hand and pressed his mouth against her ear. "This may take more than one visit. If we push too hard, they may not let us in the door again."

Tamping down her impatience, she bit her tongue. A conservatively dressed young woman approached them from the inner office and extended her hand. "Hello, I'm Haley Dean. Please come join me in my office. Maybe I can help you."

"Thank you," Michelina said, impressed with the calm the woman projected as the three of them entered an office decorated in peaceful shades of blue that reminded her of the waters surrounding Marceau.

"Please take a seat. Did I understand that you're interested in the Costa Rica project?" Ms. Dean asked as she pulled a file folder from a drawer next to her desk. "Here is the prospectus. I'll be happy to answer any questions you may have."

"I appreciate your willingness to talk with us, and I'm certain you know the ins and outs of this deal, but I have this quirk about preferring to talk with the person who draws the bottom line," Jared said, sinking into an upholstered chair. "What will it take for us to meet with Jack Raven?"

Haley Dean smiled. "Today it would take an international flight."

Michelina's heart sank in disappointment. "He's not here?"

"No, I'm sorry. He's a very busy man. Sometimes I think I spend more time on rescheduling his appointments than on anything else."

Michelina saw her opportunity to meet Jack Raven slipping through her fingertips. Desperation twisted through her. She glanced around the room. "Will he be back in town soon?"

"Oh, he's usually in this office two or three days a week, unless he finds an opportunity he has to move on immediately." She smiled and clicked the mouse for her laptop computer. "That's what happened today. The soonest I can schedule you would be in two months."

"Oh, that's too late," Michelina said.

Jared took her hand in a comforting gesture. "Are you sure there isn't something sooner? Maybe we could fly to meet him somewhere."

Michelina's gaze fell on a plaque of recognition from a charitable organization hanging on the wall.

"Um, I actually think I may have met Jack before. At a charity function."

Haley Dean hesitated, and some of her warmth seemed to fade. "Really? Where?"

"In New York," Michelina improvised.

Ms. Dean gave Michelina and Jared a long, speculative glance. "I'll give Jack your names when he returns, and perhaps he will be able to see you sooner."

Michelina stifled a groan of frustration. "Oh, I doubt he would remember me. There were so many people at that function," she said. It wasn't exactly a lie—there had been a real function, not a charity fundraiser but her formal christening.

"I think you underestimate yourself. You're quite beautiful, and very memorable, I'm sure."

Michelina looked into Haley Dean's eyes and glimpsed a flash of protectiveness and something deeper in the gaze of Jack's assistant. Realization seeped into her. Haley Dean was a total tiger where her boss was concerned. Michelina suspected Haley was in love with Jack. Best not to alienate her.

She sighed and turned toward Jared. "Well, darling," she said, and forced herself to continue with a straight face despite Jared's uplifted eyebrow. "I believe we are at the mercy of Mrs. Dean."

"Miss," Haley corrected. "I'll do what I can, but you should know that Mr. Raven just doesn't have time for many face-to-face appointments."

Does he have eyes like mine? Is there any chance that he's my brother? Michelina wanted to ask, but she didn't want to blow her chances.

"Maybe a night at the opera will console you," Jared said, his gaze full of tenderness and amusement at her game. She sensed he knew how important this was to her. Handing Haley Dean his card, he informed her, "I can be reached on my cell at any time."

Resisting the urge to beg or demand, because she suspected it would do no good, Michelina allowed Jared to guide her out of the building. He helped her into his truck and climbed in on the driver's side. "'Darling'?" he asked, referring to the endearment she'd called him just moments before.

"Well, I had to do something. I think Haley Dean thought I had romantic designs on Jack."

Jared did a double take. "How in the world did you get that impression?"

She waved her hand in a dismissive gesture. "It's a woman thing. I could see it in her eyes. She's in love with him."

Jared dropped his jaw. "How do you know?"

"I just do. I looked into her eyes and I saw something, and then I just knew. I figured if I called you darling, she might relax and try to get us in to see Jack. For Pete's sake, I think it would be easier to get in to see the queen."

"And have you seen the queen?" he asked, starting the ignition.

She automatically opened her mouth to say yes, then snapped her mouth shut. "At a public appearance once. So, do we go back to the ranch now?"

He shook his head. "Didn't you hear me? We're going to the opera."

Surprise and pleasure rushed through her. "We are? You weren't pretending?"

He shook his head and glanced at her. "I'm the real thing," he said, leaving the car in Park. "What you see is what you get. What about you?"

Her stomach clenched at the expression on his face. He might have asked his question in a casual tone, but he wanted answers. She'd seen the questions in his eyes before, but brushed them aside. He wouldn't always allow her to, though. She sensed the time was coming when Jared would demand answers to his questions. And Michelina didn't know what she would do then.

"You know everything important about me," she assured him. "You know things about me that no one else does."

"I want to know more," he said, the easiness in his voice completely gone. "I want to know where you were born. Where your family lives, and what they do and how all that has affected you."

She bit her lip and held her breath.

Jared reached out and pulled her against him. "I know your body, but I want to know your mind, Mimi. I want to know more."

Michelina felt her throat tighten over a sudden lump of emotion. She wanted him to know her. She wanted to tell him the truth, but she was so frightened....

"Mimi?"

"I'm afraid."

"Why?"

"I'm afraid that once you know about my background, all your feelings for me will change. I just can't stand the thought of that.''

His eyebrows furrowed in confusion. "Is your family in the Mafia or something?"

She gave a short laugh. "No, although they may feel like it at times. No, they're just dysfunctional." She searched for a way to answer some of his questions without telling him everything. "The family business is very demanding. Everyone is expected to contribute to it in some way."

"How do you contribute?" he asked.

Michelina's stomach twisted again. "I haven't really made my contribution yet. That's in my future." She thought of the man her family expected her to marry and felt so trapped she could barely breathe.

"You don't sound happy about it."

"I'm not sure I have a choice."

He cradled her jaw with his hand so she would meet his gaze. "You always have a choice, duchess. The choices may not be perfect and the consequences may not be fun, but you always have a choice."

In Jared's world, she would have choices, she thought. In Jared's world, her life could be different. She could be more than Princess Useless. The relentless sense of family obligation, however, had been drilled into her at a young age, and Michelina didn't know if she was strong enough to completely turn her back on her family. She wasn't certain she could live with the guilt.

"Could we please take a break from this subject?"

He nodded slowly, and she knew the questions would come again.

* * *

When Michelina complained that she had nothing appropriate to wear to the opera, Jared stopped at Denver's Cherry Creek Mall and she selected a dress, bag and shoes in no time flat. Jared was impressed.

Michelina just smiled. Shopping was one of the few skills she'd been allowed to hone over the years. After the shopping expedition, Jared checked them into a suite at Brown's Palace and Michelina marveled over the period decor.

She made no apologies for commandeering one of the large bathrooms. She wanted to look her absolute best. For once in her life—and a secret part of her feared she would only have this once—she wanted to knock Jared McNeil off his feet.

The way her hands trembled slightly as she applied her eyeliner surprised her. Michelina couldn't remember being nervous ever before when getting ready to meet a man. Her heart tripped over itself. She had been on too many chaperoned dates to count, but this was her first real date with Jared. Crazy though it might seem, especially considering the fact that they were already lovers, she wanted him to be impressed. She applied her lipstick, smudging it by accident, and swore.

She brushed her hair and stared into the mirror. She looked the same as she had just a few weeks ago before she'd left Marceau, but she knew she was oh, so different. Taking a calming breath, she smoothed the pink silk dress over her hips and left the bathroom. She turned the corner to the living area of the suite and came face-to-face with Jared.

Oh, wow. She gaped at him. She'd seen him in casual clothes and jeans and…well, nothing, but she hadn't been prepared for how he would look in a black suit. The rancher had disappeared. In his place stood a man sophisticated, confident, devastating to her knees. The only thing that saved her was the fact that he hadn't blinked since he'd seen her.

"Good Lord," he muttered. "I had a hard enough time pulling the men off you when you wore a pony-tail, sunglasses and jeans. If you'd dressed like this for the county celebration, you would have caused a riot."

She wanted to cause a riot in *him.* "I'll take that as a compliment," she said, smiling up at him. "You look quite amazing yourself."

His lips twitched and he glanced down at his suit. "You expected me to wear overalls?"

"I don't know what I expected, but this is the first time I've seen you in a suit, and…"

"And?" he prompted.

"And Mr. McNeil-with-the-ego-so-big-I-don't-need-to-stroke-it, you take my breath away."

"Is that so?" he said, looking incredibly pleased with himself. He slid his hand behind her neck and, stroking her nape, lowered his mouth to hers.

She drank in the sensation of the kiss, savoring his flavor and the subtle scent of his aftershave. She could get addicted to the way he smelled, the way he felt, the way he kissed her.

Jared pulled back and sucked in a sharp breath. "We need to go before I try to talk you out of that dress."

Michelina lifted her fingers to his lips to rub off
her lipstick. He caught her hand and slid her thumb
inside his mouth. She immediately felt a rush of heat.
''When does the show start?'' she asked breathlessly.

He swore and tugged her toward the door. ''Don't
look at me that way.''

''What way?'' she asked, having trouble keeping
her steps steady.

''Like you'd let me take you right this minute
dressed or undressed,'' he muttered, punching the
button for the elevator.

''Oops. I guess I'd better not look at you then,''
she said, and stepped into the elevator. ''Because
you're reading me like a book.''

He made a sound of sexual frustration and pulled
her into his arms, resting his forehead against hers.
''You're going to be the death of me.''

''I don't want to be the death of you,'' she protested. ''I just want to make you feel a little…both-
ered.''

He rolled his eyes and pulled her lower body
against his, making her intimately aware of his
arousal. ''If this is bothered, you've succeeded.''

He kissed her again and didn't stop until the elevator doors flew open and the guests waiting in the
lobby started to giggle. Hot with more than embarrassment, she allowed him to guide her out of the
lobby to the arts center where the opera *Carmen* was
being presented.

They took their seats in a private balcony box.
''Very nice seats. I'm glad I don't have to share

you," she said. "How did you manage this on such short notice?"

He shrugged. "I have a few connections."

She leaned back in her seat and smiled at the way he didn't try to impress her with his background or *connections*.

He met her gaze. "Why the smile?"

"I was just thinking that you're very different from the other men I've dated. They often try to impress me with who they know or their titles or—"

"Well, you know my job title. Rancher."

Michelina had meant other kinds of titles, but she had no intention of correcting him. "And mayor," she said.

He gave a heavy sigh. "Interim mayor," he corrected. "And that's under duress."

"Uncle is another of your titles. Brother."

He nodded.

"Lover," she whispered. "My lover."

His eyes darkened. "I thought I told you not to look at me that way."

"I can't not look at you this way."

He closed his eyes and shook his head. "This is going to be a long night." He sat back in his seat and slid his arm around her shoulders.

The best singers in the world might have been singing the roles of Carmen and Don José but Jared couldn't keep his hands or eyes off Mimi. The sound of her laughter crawled under his skin and went straight to his heart. He liked the way she leaned into him as if her trust for him were instinctive and total.

The knowledge, however, that Mimi's trust for him was incomplete was like a rock he couldn't remove from his shoe. It bothered him. A lot.

He wasn't sure when it had happened, but somewhere along the way, he'd grown to care for her more than he'd intended. More than her laughter had gotten under his skin, and that was bad news, because as sure as the wind blew in Wyoming, Mimi wouldn't be staying. The thought of it made him feel like he had a case of permanent indigestion.

He had a gut feeling she would be leaving soon, and he was struggling with the need to have more laughter, more fights, more making up, more helping her to see all she was capable of…more of Mimi. She'd been a pain in the butt and caused more than her share of chaos, but she'd also lit up his house, and he wasn't ready to go back to his quiet, peaceful, Mimi-free life yet.

Following an unbidden impulse, Jared reached for her and took her mouth.

She gave a little gasp of surprise before she surrendered to the kiss. He slid his hand to her jaw and savored the texture of her silky hair and velvet skin against his fingers. Her mouth was sweet and responsive. She took him by surprise when she slid her tongue past his lips, taunting him to respond.

He felt his temperature climb as she continued the sexy sweep of her tongue over his. When he returned the caress, she tilted her head to give him better access and drew his tongue into her mouth, as if she couldn't get enough of him. He grew hard.

"You're getting me hot," he whispered against her mouth.

"You started it," she retorted, sucking at his lower lip.

His gaze dipped over the tops of her breasts when he felt her pressing against his chest. He knew how she felt in his hands, in his mouth. "I thought you were excited about seeing the opera."

"What opera?" she asked, sliding her hands beneath his coat to caress his chest.

The strength of his arousal rocked through his veins like gasoline. He wanted inside. He wanted to know all her secrets, all her fears. He wanted her out of her clothes, flat on her back with her legs wrapped around his waist while he sank into her wet, tight femininity.

When she slid one of her hands to his thigh, it was all he could do not to pull her onto his lap. He tore his mouth from hers and sucked in what he hoped would be a mind-clearing breath. Instead, he inhaled the scent of her perfume spiced with her desire. He clamped his hand over hers as it wandered up his thigh.

"We're going to get arrested if we don't stop."

She looked up at him, her eyes nearly black with arousal. "I don't want to stop. I don't ever want to stop with you."

Jared's chest tightened. He wondered how she managed to grab him by the heart and crotch at the same time. "Don't you want to see the rest of the opera?"

The slow shake of her head ripped his restraint. That was it. He wasn't asking again. Standing, he helped her to her feet and ushered her out of their private box to the lobby.

The cool night air did nothing to bring his heat under control. They walked the short distance to their hotel in silence, her hand firmly clasped in his.

As soon as the elevator doors tucked just the two of them inside, they fell into each others' arms. Jared wasn't sure what drove him. The knowledge that Mimi would be slipping through his fingers like water soon? The wildly primitive urge to possess her the same way she had begun to possess him? On her lips, he tasted the same combination of passion and desperation that throbbed inside him.

He lowered his mouth to her throat, then to the top of one of her breasts. She tugged down the strap of her dress, baring her breast to his gaze, to his mouth.

The bold invitation made him want to take her against the wall. He dropped his mouth to her nipple, drawing it deep into his mouth. The sensation of the stiff peak on his tongue drove him crazy.

Her moan tore through him. His restraint evaporated like beads of water on a hot griddle. He slid one of his hands up the slit of her dress and beneath the silk piece of nothing. She was so hot, so wet, so sweet. He plunged his finger inside her and felt her clench around him.

"Jared," she said, her voice pleading.

The elevator doors whisked open, and he instinctively stepped in front of her, shielding her from any potential prying eyes. He adjusted her dress and led her to the suite. The second he closed the door, they were all over each other again.

He pushed down her dress. She pulled loose his tie and struggled with his buttons. She let out a husky litany of frustrated oaths in the sexiest voice he'd ever heard. Jared obliged her by ripping his dress shirt apart, sending the buttons flying.

Mimi blinked. "That was impressive."

"I'm motivated," he muttered, the sensation of her bare skin against his driving him more crazy than he'd been before.

"There is something that I've wondered about," she ventured, unfastening his slacks and sliding her small hand around his erection.

Jared thought he might explode. Taking a quick, shallow breath, he couldn't stop himself from pushing into her caress. "What have you been wondering about?"

Her eyes smoky with desire, she bit her lip. "I wondered what it would be like with, uh, me on top."

An immediate visual of Mimi, her hair flowing over him, her breasts pressed into him, as she rode him seared him. Jared was so hot he knew steam was going to start rising from his body any minute. He kissed her, and the power of his want and need for her was so strong, he felt it in his bones. He wanted Mimi in every possible way. He wanted her so much despite the fact that the end of their relationship was imminent and the fall was going to be rough. Any man in his right mind would take the pleasure and seal off his heart, but for Jared, half measures with Mimi weren't possible anymore.

"You're not saying anything," Mimi said.

"You've fried my brain."

Her lips lifted in a smile that grabbed his heart and twisted. ''I keep trying to knock you off your feet.''

''Oh, duchess, you did that a long time ago.'' He kissed her and made her bra and panties disappear. Then his pants disappeared, too. He wasn't sure how. She'd probably melted them. They kissed their way to the large bed.

He touched her body and she touched his, and for once, he made himself totally open to her. He felt her sigh against his chest as she explored his muscles and ribs. He knew he was strong, but she made him aware of it in a totally different way.

She pressed her open mouth against his throat in a caress that he cherished. She was silky, slow-moving, and quiet except for her breath. The silence, however, was the noisiest thing he'd ever experienced. She didn't verbally say she was awed by him, but her hands did. She didn't announce how much she wanted him, but the way her body sought his sang it to him over and over again. She didn't say she loved him, but her eyes shouted it.

And when she rode him with her hair flowing around her shoulders, Jared locked his gaze with hers and knew he would never be the same.

Eleven

Michelina awakened early and drank in the sight of Jared's face. His hard bone structure was barely softened by sleep. She remembered the way he had possessed her last night. And the way she had possessed him.

Her heart contracted. Who would have thought Princess Useless could have such a powerful effect on such a powerful man? The sex between them was more than physical. It was as if what was going on inside them was too big to contain and it had to find expression.

But it was temporary. The unwelcome thought felt like a poison dart in the middle of a beautiful moment. Suddenly too restless to sit still, she slid carefully out of bed, half-surprised she didn't wake up Jared. He was usually awake before her. She padded into the living area and pulled on yesterday's jeans and T-shirt.

Looking down onto the nearly empty street below with her mind full of Jared, she thought of how much he had given her. She'd never dreamed she could feel so confident, so full of possibilities. She wanted to give him something. The man didn't appear to need anything, and he wasn't the type to get excited over a gold watch. She frowned in concentration, her gaze drifting over pots of colorful flowers. An idea came to mind. She dismissed it, then returned to it, fidgeting with the draperies.

He would probably think it was bloody silly, she warned herself, but then again, he might not. Following her impulse, she splashed water on her face, brushed her teeth and hair, skipped her shoes in favor of speed and took the elevator to the lobby.

The gift shop was closed, but she didn't let that stop her. It took a few minutes, but she successfully cajoled the front desk clerk into opening the shop just for her. She made her purchase, paid with cash from her pocket and headed for the elevator with three roses in her hand.

The sound of a familiar foreign accent caught her attention just as she rounded the corner, and she looked over her shoulder. Her stomach fell to her feet. She quickly hid behind the wall and sneaked one more glance at the reception area.

She saw two men talking to the clerk who'd just helped her. Her heart sank as she confirmed her earlier thought that she recognized one of them. He was with Marceau palace security. They were here to collect her, she knew. They were here to collect the prodigal princess and take her back to where she belonged.

Everything inside her rebelled at the prospect. Lifting a hand to her throat, she felt herself shake so hard, she wondered if the floor was moving. But it wasn't. More like walls crashing down on her. Panic roared through her. She had to get to Jared, and then she had to disappear. She pushed the elevator button and thanked heaven when the doors immediately opened.

Once inside, she closed her eyes to keep from hyperventilating. The sweet scent of the roses combined with the bitter taste of regret in her throat. She wasn't ready to go back yet. Sure, it had been nearly a month, but it had gone by in the blink of an eye. And she was determined to try to get an appointment with Jake Raven. How could she accomplish that if she was forced to return to Marceau?

Her head spinning, she tried to form an explanation for Jared, but her pitiful brain couldn't put two words together. The elevator reached her floor, and she broke into a cold sweat.

Jared heard what sounded like fumbling with the lock on the door, then a feminine oath. Recognizing the voice even through the door, he chuckled. Mimi. He'd heard her leave earlier and had thought about going after her, but he figured she wouldn't be gone long, since she'd left her shoes.

Curious and amused, he opened the door. She was swearing at her key card in one hand and holding roses in the other. She stopped swearing and met his gaze. His heart turned over.

"Roses?"

"They're for you," she said, thrusting him into his hand as she swept past him and pulled the door closed.

Jared glanced down at three red roses, floored by the romantic gift. His insides melted, while the rest of him turned stiff. He shook his head, searching for an adequate response. "This is a first. I—uh—"

"That's what I was hoping. I wanted to give you something no one else had."

"You already did that," he said, touching one of the soft petals. It reminded him of her skin. "You gave me yourself."

"It didn't seem like enough."

"It was," he said, then grinned. "But these are lovely, too." He looked at her again and suddenly saw the tightness around her mouth. She was pale. Her frustration with the lock and the flowers had distracted him, but now he recognized her distress. "What's the matter?"

She took a deep breath and bit her lip. "I don't know how to say this."

Jared's stomach sank. There was never good news after the kind of statement she'd just made. "I can't help you if you can't tell me."

Her eyes flashed with anger, and she pushed her hair behind her ear in a savage gesture as she began to pace. "I've been found," she said bitterly. "I saw someone connected with my family in the lobby while I was getting the roses, and I know they're looking for me. They'll probably either be up here any minute, or just lying in wait in the lobby. Jared, I'm just not ready to go back there yet. I can't.''

She looked like a caged animal. ''What do you want me to do?''

''I don't know. I don't know what to do.'' She turned toward him midpace. ''They must know I've been with you or they wouldn't have been able to find me here, so I can't go back to the ranch. I'm just not ready to go back. I need to disappear for a little longer, but I want to try to see Jack Raven.''

Jared ignored the knots forming in his gut and throat. ''You could go to Colorado Springs. It's not that far, but maybe far enough to buy you some time and still give you access to Denver.''

She lifted her fingers to either side of her forehead as if trying to concentrate despite the panic written on her face. ''I'll need a vehicle. And I'm running out of money,'' she murmured to herself.

Shades of his ex-fiancée, Jennifer, floated eerily through his mind, but he tried to push the thought aside. Mimi looked as if she were ready to cry. ''I can give you some money and you can use my truck.'' The second offer caused him some misgivings, which he again tried to push aside.

She looked at him in surprise. ''You'd let me use your truck?''

''Yeah,'' he said with a shrug. ''You'd bring it back, wouldn't you?''

''Of course,'' she said.

''But I think it's about time you told me the real story about your family.'' He gave her a serious look.

She looked away and her shoulders slumped. ''Do

I have to?'' She waved her hand. ''Don't answer that. I know I do.'' She sighed, then turned to face him. ''Would you do one more thing before I tell you?''

''What?'' he asked, thinking she had no idea how much he would do for her. He wondered if his gut would ever feel normal again.

She walked closer to him. ''Would you kiss me?''

The knots inside him tangled again. This scene had all the signs of *goodbye*. He'd known this moment would come sometime, he reminded himself. He'd even known it would come soon. He just hadn't expected to feel as if a ton of bricks had been dumped on his head. Hating the painful knot in his throat, he swallowed hard. ''Sure, I'll kiss you, duchess,'' he said, and pulled her into his arms.

This time she took his mouth and kissed him as if there was no tomorrow. Maybe there wasn't. Her lips were sweet and passionate, full of want and need, desperate. He tasted the same metallic taste of desperation on his own tongue, but tried to focus on how she felt in his arms, her vibrant energy. His heart pounded hard against his rib cage.

The kiss went on and on as if neither of them had the will to end it. Finally they both took a breath. She lifted her hands to his face and looked deep into his eyes. ''I want to memorize the way you are right now, the way you're looking at me, because you'll never look at me that way again,'' she said.

His chest felt so tight, he found it difficult to breathe.

She took a step back and composed herself with effort. His hands burned to pull her against him again.

She sighed and looked away from him. "My family name is Dumont. We live in a small island country named Marceau off the coast of France."

"Okay," Jared said. The name and the country were vaguely familiar, although he couldn't quite place them. That explained the strange accent that crept into her language every now and then. "So Deerman isn't your real name."

"That's right. My given name is Michelina Catherine." She paused, and he saw a look of sheer dread on her face.

Nothing earthshaking so far, though, he thought. She wasn't from a Mafia family, and she wasn't claiming to be an alien from Mars. He started to wonder if she'd overblown the situation in her mind. "Okay," he said. "So you and your family live near France. None of this sounds over-the-top to me."

She winced. "My family doesn't just live in Marceau. We run it," she said. "We rule it."

Rule. Jared's mind slammed into the word at a hundred miles per hour. "Rule?"

She nodded. "My mother is Queen Anna Catherine. My oldest brother, Michel, is heir to the throne. My next brother, Auguste, is military chief. My third brother, Nicholas, is a doctor who advises the Secretary of Health. My fourth brother, Alexander, operates a yacht-building business and lives part-time in North Carolina."

Jared stared at her. He didn't know what he'd expected, but it hadn't been this.

"The plan is for all of us to fulfill a royal role in one way or another."

Jared felt as if his brain was a tire spinning fruitlessly without progress in a snowdrift. "So you're a princess?"

She sighed and folded her hands together. "Yes."

He scratched his head as he tried to piece together everything she'd told him. "If you don't mind my asking, what is your role?"

Her face flattened to an expressionless mask. "To marry a count from Italy, bear children and provide photo ops for the press."

His heart stopped. "You're engaged?"

She shook her head. "My mother, the queen, has told me that she would like me to marry this man. For the good of Marceau," she said with a slightly ill expression on her face.

"But you don't want to."

"I'm not supposed to think about what I want."

Despite his own raging emotions, Jared couldn't prevent the surge of a feeling of protectiveness for Mimi— Michelina, he mentally corrected himself. He walked toward her and took her shoulders in his hands. "If *you* don't think about what you want, then nobody will."

"But I was born to serve. I was born to fulfill a duty."

"Do you have to serve this way?"

She opened her mouth, then hesitated and closed it. "I always thought I did…until I met you." She closed her eyes and shook her head. "I can't think about this right now. I must go, or I won't even get the opportunity to meet my brother."

Jared could practically see her turmoil bubbling up

from inside her. He despised the helplessness he felt. "If you need something, call me."

Her gaze flashed. "Don't say that!"

"What do you mean?"

"I mean, don't say that! I don't deserve it. I've deceived you and I'm sorry. I don't deserve your generosity." Her eyes filled with tears. "I don't deserve the use of your truck. I don't deserve anything from you." She audibly swallowed a sob. "I can't give you anything back."

Jared's head and chest hurt worse than when he'd gotten a concussion and broken rib playing football in high school. He ground his teeth against the unwelcome emotions ripping at him. Mimi—Michelina, he corrected himself again—was headed for hysteria land, if she wasn't already there. Practicality offered an island of relief from the intense emotions colliding with both of them right now.

"Listen, you've got to get hold of yourself if you're going to be driving my truck."

She sniffed and looked at him in confusion.

"You're not used to driving on the freeway, and your family will likely kill me if anything happens to you while you're driving my vehicle. If you really want some more time before you go back to the royal penitentiary, then you need to focus."

She sniffed again. "On what?"

"On getting your stuff together, following my directions and accomplishing your goals."

She blinked, stiffening her spine before his very eyes. "You're right. I can't wallow over being Princess Useless. That would truly be useless."

He frowned. "Princess Useless?"

She curled her lip in disgust and headed for the bedroom. "My nickname for myself."

While Michelina hastily packed her belongings, Jared shut out all kinds of unwelcome emotions and wrote out the directions to Colorado Springs. As she reentered the room, he detached the truck keys from his key ring.

He reluctantly met her gaze and tried to remain unmoved by the turbulence he saw in her eyes. "Follow the directions, and don't go over the speed limit. If you get stopped by the police, the registration is in the glove compartment. Here's my cell," he said, handing over his mobile phone.

Her eyes widened. "But you need that."

"You need it worse than I do," he said bluntly. "You're traveling in a foreign country without a guide. I wrote my pager and home phone on the directions, in case you get in over your head."

"That's what you expect, isn't it? That I'll get in over my head." She sighed. "That's what I've done so far."

"I'm gonna tell you something, duch—" He broke off and corrected himself, feeling an odd pluck of dry humor. "—Princess, you don't have time to feel sorry for yourself. If you've got the palace hounds nipping at your heels, you'd better get moving."

Her eyes shiny with unshed tears, she bit her lip and lifted her chin. "No such thing as a Wyoming wuss," she whispered.

"Right," he said, determined to keep it light even though he felt as if he had a tennis-ball-size knot in his throat. He chucked her chin with his forefinger. "And once you've lived in Wyoming, it never quite leaves you."

She swallowed audibly. "Thank you for everything."

He crammed his hands into his pockets to keep from reaching out to her. If he touched her, he knew she would break apart. It was a kindness that killed him, but she needed something different than an embrace from him. He handed her his hat, then opened the door. "Stuff your hair underneath that and try the service elevator."

She plopped his hat on her head and breezed toward the elevator. "I'll pay you back," she said, throwing him a kiss.

"Sure you will," he said, though he was anything but sure.

During the next twenty minutes, Jared told his mind to stop thinking about Michelina as he went through the motions of packing his bag. He called a dealership and made arrangements to lease a truck for one month. He figured if he didn't see Michelina or his truck again, that would give him time to buy a new vehicle. Silly, he told himself. He'd known he was kissing his truck goodbye when he handed over his keys to her.

An empty feeling gnawed at him clear down to his bones as he left the room. He instinctively inhaled, trying to catch the last of Michelina's scent. *Stop torturing yourself.* He closed the door behind him and entered the elevator. The ride down to the lobby gave him time to remember how it had felt to hold her in his arms just last night.

Grinding his teeth, he checked out of the hotel and turned to leave the building. Two men stepped directly in his path.

"Pardon me. Are you Jared McNeil?" one of the men asked.

"Who wants to know?" he demanded, but the man's accent gave him away. He looked like a high-class bouncer.

"Of course," the man said with a stiff nod. "My name is Henri Newport and this is Jean Huguenot. We're looking for this woman." Henri pulled out a photo of Michelina.

Jared's chest tightened, but he'd played poker often enough to hide his reaction.

"We understand she has been seen with you."

Protectiveness roared through him. He covered his tension by giving a low whistle. "She's a babe," he said casually. "Who is she?"

Henri looked affronted. "She is Princess Michelina Dumont of Marceau." Henri narrowed his eyes. "But you already know this. I demand you tell us where she is this instant, or there will be unpleasant consequences."

"I'd like to help you, but I can't," he said with a shrug. "I wouldn't mind meeting her, though, if you can arrange an introduction. I don't think I've ever been formally introduced to a real princess before."

Henri sputtered. "You've met her already. The desk clerk said she was with you last night."

Jared laughed. "I wish. I had a *hired* date last

night,'' he said, and winked. ''If you know what I mean. The woman I was with had long dark hair, but she was no princess.''

Jean frowned. ''You're sure?'' he said. ''You're absolutely sure you haven't seen Princess Michelina? She's been—'' Henri's nudge cut him off. ''We are concerned for her safety and well-being.''

Suffocation cloaked in words of *concern*. Jared visualized a net being thrown over Michelina's head, a cell door slamming closed with her locked inside. ''Sorry, buds, but I told you I've never been formally introduced to a princess in my life.'' And he hadn't, Jared thought, as he left the men staring after him in confusion. He hadn't been formally introduced to Michelina. He'd made love to her, but it would be better for everyone if he could find a way to forget her.

Twelve

Two weeks later, Jared trudged up the porch steps. It was late and he'd skipped dinner again. His stomach protested with a growl. His objective had been simple—to work so hard and so long, he couldn't even think about Michelina, let alone miss her.

Walking through the front door, he felt the familiar ache in his chest and sighed. So far, he hadn't accomplished his objective. He petted Leo before he stopped in the kitchen, where he put together a sandwich and pulled a beer from the refrigerator. In no mood to sit in the den and watch television or do paperwork, he decided to eat his late snack on his way upstairs, then hit the shower.

His contrary mind wandered as he ate half his sandwich without tasting it, and he speculated about what Michelina was doing tonight. He wondered if she had gotten past Jack Raven's gatekeepers, if she'd returned to Marceau, if she'd wrecked his truck. He took a long swig of beer and frowned. *She* wasn't his business.

Everything inside him rebelled at the thought, but he had to get used to it. Eating the other half of his sandwich, he walked into his darkened bedroom and didn't bother to turn on the light as he passed through to the master bath.

As much as he had fought to avoid getting tangled in Michelina's web, even though he'd known she would create chaos in his life, he'd been unable to resist her. Underneath her privileged exterior beat the heart of a female warrior. She'd been determined to overcome her limitations. She'd wanted to fence, accepted his challenge to swim, met him toe-to-toe with her determination. Even though she'd been frightened, she'd jumped into the lake and rescued that toddler. Even though she'd been a virgin, she'd burned up his bed and all his defenses.

She was the most exciting woman he'd ever met, and he felt as if the light had gone out in his life ever since she'd left. Taking another long swallow of beer, he stripped out of his clothes, wondering how long it would take before he felt normal again. How long would it be before he didn't think of her every minute he wasn't working and every other minute when he was working? How long before he didn't reach for her in the morning and wonder what she'd gotten into while he'd been working in the afternoon?

He'd liked the way she'd trusted him with her body and with confidences she hadn't shared with other people, even her family. He'd started to have a strange feeling of destiny about her. It was crazy as hell, but it was as if he'd been intended to come into her life, and she in his. She'd gotten him out of his funk, made him laugh…and made him feel alive.

He turned on the jets of the shower and stepped inside, swearing. Only he would fall head over butt for a princess, for Pete's sake. Talk about impossible! He stood under the spray and tried to focus on anything but Michelina. Romeo's stud schedule. His recent success at finding a new mayoral candidate to replace him. Getting another stud and building another barn. Maybe if Jared crammed his brain full enough, he would fall asleep and dream about the ranch instead of her.

Staying in the shower an extra couple of minutes, Jared savored the hot spray. He reluctantly got out, dried off, wrapped a towel around his waist and walked into the bedroom. He opened a drawer to pull out some boxers.

''Surprise,'' a feminine voice said from behind him.

Jared stopped cold. He shook his head, certain he was imagining things. He swore under his breath. Now he was having delusions. Turning around to confirm his insanity, he saw Michelina sitting on his bed.

His heart tripped over itself, and he blinked repeatedly. An apparition, he told himself, walking toward the bed. He would reach out to touch her and feel air, nothing else.

He extended his hand, and she looked at him uncertainly. ''Jared?'' She lifted her own hand and enclosed his.

Jared stared down at their entwined fingers in disbelief.

''You don't look happy to see me,'' she said, tugging as if to pull her hand away.

No chance, Jared thought, tightening his grip. ''I'm surprised.'' He shook his head, staring at her, taking in the sight of the face, the eyes, the woman who had haunted him relentlessly. ''I didn't expect to see you again.''

She frowned. ''I told you I would return the truck. You didn't believe me.''

Her pride flashed before him, and he chuckled. If this was a delusion, it was a doozy. ''I didn't count on it after Henri and Jean cornered me in the lobby at the hotel.''

Her eyes widened. ''Oh, no. They didn't hurt you, did they?''

''No, I made up a story about a woman who looked kinda like you but wasn't you, and didn't give them a chance to argue.'' He sank down onto the bed. ''So you brought back the truck,'' he said, bracing himself for the possibility that she would be leaving again in a few minutes.

''The good news is that I didn't wreck it. But I did change the color.''

''The color?''

''Yes, it's no longer green. Now it's black. I was afraid the palace might be looking for a green truck. But I couldn't do anything about the license plate except put mud on it.''

Impressed with her ingenuity, he nodded in approval. "Good move."

"You don't mind that I had your truck painted a different color?" she asked.

She could have painted it purple with pink polka dots as long as he got another chance to look at her. "Nah. What about Jack?"

She made a face. "I tried too many times to count, but he was either not there or not available. I even tried dressing as part of the janitorial staff, but they caught me and threw me out. They threatened me with legal action if I didn't stop," she said indignantly.

"I'm sorry, Michelina. I don't know what to tell you," Jared said, surprised at how the sound of her voice made him feel five years younger. "Maybe after you go back to Marceau—"

"That's another thing," she said, interrupting him, squeezing his hand and biting her lip in an obvious display of nerves. "I've had a lot of time to think, and I need to tell you—"

His heart twisted, and he shook his head. "You don't have to tell me anything. I know you've got to go back."

"That's just it. I'm *not* going back. I want to stay with you."

His heart flew at the same time that his mind rejected her words. Unable to stop himself a minute longer, he pulled her into his arms. "Sweetheart, you don't know how much that means to me, but I know you've got to go back. I did a little research on Marceau while you were gone, and you're important to your family and to your country.''

''But what about what *I* want? You've always told me I have a choice.''

''Yeah, but—''

''Are you saying you don't want me?''

''Hell, no.''

''Jared, I've made a decision. I'm willing to give up my title to be with you.''

All Jared could do was stare at her. His heart, his lungs, his brain ceased to function. He'd told himself not to expect to see her again. He wondered if he was dreaming.

Her lip quivered. ''You're not saying anything.'' She ducked her head and covered her eyes with her hand. ''I just realized I've been a bit presumptuous,'' she said with a forced chuckle that sounded more like a sob. ''I've been so focused on figuring out what *I* wanted that I didn't think about what *you* want, and what you want might not be me.''

Jared forced his mouth to work. ''You know I want you.''

She still didn't look at him. ''But you might not want me the same way I want you.''

''What way do you want me, Michelina?'' he asked, putting her hand aside and guiding her chin upward so she would meet his gaze.

''I want you always,'' she whispered.

His heart nearly burst. ''Aw, hell,'' he said, squeezing the bridge of his nose.

She ripped her hand away from him. ''I was afraid of that,'' she wailed. ''I was afraid you would think that I'm too much trouble, that I was fun for a while, but not—''

He covered her mouth. ''Would you just shut up for a minute so I can catch my freakin' breath? I didn't expect ever to see you again, then I find you in my bed telling me you want to be with me always. I feel like I'm having some kind of out-of-body experience—that I don't want to end,'' he added emphatically.

''I gotta think about this,'' he said, rising from the bed, his mind moving like sludge. ''I can't let you give up your title.'' He shook his head. Everything inside him rebelled at the thought.

''But—''

He held up a hand to silence her, then raked his fingers through his wet hair. ''There's gotta be another way. There's gotta be …'' He sighed. ''Your family. I don't think you've thought this all the way through.''

She sprang to her feet. ''Yes, I have. You told me not to fight my purpose. My purpose is to be with you. I've never accomplished more or felt so useful as I have with you. You make me be a better person.''

Her passionate response tugged at his heartstrings. ''Oh, Michelina, you were always a better person. You just didn't know it.''

''You showed me. I have to be with you. I have never been more sure of anything in my life.''

She was scared, but damn determined. He could read it in her eyes. He took her hand. ''How can you turn your back on your family?''

Her eyes darkened with sadness. ''I don't want to,

but I can't give up my life to marry someone I don't love for the sake of good PR for Marceau.'' She looked up at him and touched his face. ''I always thought love was something giddy and magical, but you've taught me that it's so much more.''

She flat-out humbled him. He took her into his arms and kissed her. It was a kiss of promises he made with his heart, promises he would keep. He couldn't believe she'd come back. He didn't know how they would work it all out, but they'd have to. As he felt the fire flare between them and his blood heated, Jared could only think of her. He would think of her family tomorrow.

Michelina made love to him with the force of a firestorm. He should have been dead tired, but he stayed awake all night, trying to decide on the best way to handle the situation. As much as Michelina swore she would turn her back on her family, Jared couldn't allow it. There had to be a better option.

When morning came, so did his conclusion. As he lay propped on his elbow beside her, stroking her hair, he wondered if they were strong enough for what lay ahead.

Her eyes fluttered open and she smiled, lifting her hand to his chin. Jared caught her hand in his and lifted it to his lips. ''Good morning, beautiful. We're going to Marceau.''

Michelina's smile fell. ''I was hoping for Vegas… one of those little wedding chapels they have there.''

He chuckled and shook his head. "Don't tempt me."

She sat up and the covers fell, revealing her naked breasts and torso. "But that's what I want to do."

Feeling himself harden, he stifled a groan. "You've succeeded. You are a walking, talking, breathing temptation to me. I'd like to give in to that temptation permanently. I want to be your husband." He took a careful breath, knowing this was the most important moment in his life. "Will you marry me?"

Her eyes filled with tears, and she threw her arms around him. "Yes, yes, yes. Let's go to Vegas and get married before anyone can make things difficult."

He felt a rush of euphoria tempered with the knowledge that they had a bumpy road ahead. "Do you trust me?"

"Yes," she said, pulling back slightly and meeting his gaze.

"Then we have to go to Marceau."

Dread crossed her face. "My family will make things impossible. That's why I said I was willing to give up my title."

"Yeah, but you're forgetting what I told you. Don't fight your purpose. Part of your purpose is to be a daughter, a sister, an aunt and princess. You don't have to choose between being any of those and being my wife."

She let out a sigh of relief, but her gaze was still tinged with uncertainty. "But my family will never go for this."

"If we go to Marceau and tell them our plans, they'll never say they didn't have a chance. I don't want you to have regrets. I could live with a lot, but not that.''

"I would never regret being your wife.''

Lord, he hoped not. "This is the right thing to do.''

"If you say so,'' she said doubtfully. "Make sure you pack enough antacids for both of us.''

Jared took in his surroundings as the limo traveled from the Marceau airport to the palace. Marceau was an exquisite jewel of an island, with white sandy beaches and mountains surrounded by blue, blue water. To most observers, it was a paradise no one in their right mind would ever want to leave.

Michelina, with her nails digging into his palm as she recited her family tree, was clearly the exception. "My father's name was Jules. My mother is Anna Catherine, but you can just call her Your Majesty. I can't predict which of my brothers will be the biggest problem, but Michel is a likely candidate. He's the oldest and since he's first in line for the throne, he has serious control issues. His American wife, Maggie, has really helped, but he still feels responsible for everything. He has a son named Max, from a previous marriage, and he and Maggie have just had another child, a boy with red hair like Maggie.

"Auguste stays busy with the military and his family.

"Nicholas is a wild card. He's a medical doctor, so you would think he might understand a nontraditional choice, but he's very protective when it comes to his own family. He has an American wife named Tara. She's due with their first child any minute. I'm crossing my fingers Alexander and Sophia are in North Carolina at the moment.''

Jared gently pried her fingernails from his palm and stroked her fingers to relax her. ''Will there be a quiz?'' he asked with a grin.

''How can you smile at a time like this?''

''Because I'm with the woman I love.''

She closed her eyes, and some of the tension drained out of her. She took a breath, then met his gaze. ''Promise me you won't let them change your mind about me.''

Jared looked at her in disbelief and pulled her against him. ''No chance.''

''Okay,'' she said. ''We're almost there.''

The limo rounded the corner and pulled into a driveway lined with pots of colorful flowers. The centuries-old palace stood like a proud, beautiful woman. When the driver pulled the limo to a stop, a doorman instantly appeared.

''Welcome home, Your Highness,'' he said with a slight bow as he opened Michelina's door.

''Thank you, Marc. This is Mr. Jared McNeil.''

''Welcome to Marceau, Mr. McNeil,'' Marc said, grabbing the luggage before Jared could.

Michelina took Jared's arm and looked up at him. ''Ready?''

''Whenever you are.''

''In that case, I still think Vegas sounds good.''

He tugged her forward. ''C'mon. Maybe it won't be as bad as you think.''

They walked through the palace door where four men stood waiting. They were dressed in a variety of clothes, ranging from a business suit to denims, but they all had the same silver eyes and they all wore the same facial expressions—frowns. Even Jared could have been intimidated by the four angry princes, each of whom almost matched him in height, but the strength of his feelings for Michelina made him fearless. Which could be a major mistake. He suspected he would find out soon enough.

"Welcome home, Michelina," one of the men said. "Mother is waiting to see you."

Michelina stiffened. "I've just arrived. I want to make sure my guest is made comfortable."

"We will make sure that Mr. McNeil is comfortable," her brother said smoothly. "Run along."

Jared covered a wince. Patronizing Michelina wasn't a good choice at the moment.

She stiffened further. "I'm not quite ready to run along. Jared, I'd like to introduce you to my brothers—Michel, Auguste, Nicholas and Alexander. They all answer to Your Highness," she said, smiling with effort.

"Your Highnesses," Jared said with a nod as he tried to put the best foot forward. "Nice to meet you."

Each of the men gave a brief curt nod, but said nothing.

Michelina sighed. "Where are your wives?"

"We thought it best to leave them at home."

"I disagree," she said with a sweet smile. "They civilize you."

The one she'd introduced as Nicholas unbent a smidgen and cut his eyes at her in amusement. "I can't disagree there, but Mother is waiting to see you."

"Yes, but Jared civilizes *me*."

Jared felt all four of their speculative gazes hone in on him.

"We'd like to learn his secret," Nicholas said dryly, then moved toward Michelina and embraced her. "Go on and take your guilt trip. It's already booked. We'll chat with your new friend."

"I don't trust you with him," she said bluntly.

"Afraid he can't handle us?" Nicholas goaded her.

Jared almost rose to that challenge, but he saved his firepower. He figured he would need it later.

Michelina rolled her eyes. "Okay, I'll go see Mother, but if you treat my guest with disrespect, I won't speak to any of you ever again."

"Tough threat," Nicholas said, raising his eyebrows.

"I mean it. You have him to thank for me being here right now. I wanted to go to Vegas." She turned to Jared and pressed her audacious mouth to his. Jared steadied her with his hands even as he knew she was kissing him to put her brothers on notice. At the same time, she was girding herself for her visit with her mother.

"Don't worry about me," he murmured to her. "I can handle them and ten others for you."

"My mother is the equivalent of ten others," she warned him.

He smiled and adjusted a stray strand of her hair. "So let's do the dirty work, and you can take me to the beach later."

She finally smiled, a genuine lifting of her lips that made his heart turn over. "It's a date." She strode down the hall with a world of purpose in her walk. His gaze was glued to her until she turned the corner and left his sight.

Then he turned to the four angry princes and clapped his hands together. "Show me to the rack."

Alexander, the youngest brother, almost chuckled. "No rack, but we heard you enjoy fencing, so my brothers and I thought you might enjoy a match. This way," he said, and the four of them led the way downstairs.

Jared hoped he could shake off his jet lag, or he had the uncomfortable feeling he was going to end up wearing a foil in his gut. "I'm game."

"All of us wanted to spar with you, but we knew time wouldn't permit a fencing marathon. So we drew straws, and Michel won."

Jared nodded, following them through a walkway where a beagle scampered toward them, barking and wagging his tail.

"Elvis, you scamp," Michel said, bending down to rub the dog. "My son Max's dog."

Jared knelt down to pet the squirmy animal. "Elvis?"

"My son named him," Michel said. "He drives the advisors crazy."

"Your son or Elvis?" Jared asked.

Michel threw him a sideways glance. "Elvis. Do you prefer foil?" he asked, as they entered a well-equipped fencing room.

"Yes."

"We have several changing rooms. Choose your weapon and dress out, and we can get started."

Feeling the men stare at him, he picked up a couple of foils, chose one, grabbed a suit and headed for the changing room. He knew he would need to be on guard for more than fencing. He was being tested and probed, and judging by her brothers' expressions, they hoped he'd be shipped off without Michelina. He hated to rub them the wrong way from the get-go, but if they were half as astute as Michelina, it wouldn't take them long to see that he was rock-solid set on their sister.

Minutes later, Jared stood across from Michel, his mask in place. He saluted, and the foils began to fly.

"How did you meet my sister?" Michel asked, winning a point right off the bat.

Jared instinctively protected Michelina. She already suffered from a lack of respect from her brothers—he didn't need to exacerbate that. "Her truck broke down one night near my ranch. She was stranded and was concerned about money, so I let her have one of my extra rooms for the night. When my housekeeper broke her foot the next morning, Michelina offered to help take care of my sister's daughters."

Michel faltered and Jared took advantage, tapping the prince's chest with his foil. "Michelina offered to take care of children?"

"She did a good job, diaper-changing and all."

Jared heard a roar of laughter from the sidelines, and Michel lifted his hand and called, "Time." He pushed back his mask and dipped his head in disbelief. "Michelina changed diapers?"

"Yep," Jared said, pushing back his mask. Taking a quick breath, he hazarded a glance at her other brothers. He swallowed a grin at the varying degrees of amazement he saw on their faces. "She jumped into a lake and rescued a toddler during a county celebration, which she planned, and organized a book drive. And took a few fencing lessons from me, because I understand her lessons were interrupted when she was younger. That right, Nicholas?"

Complete silence filled the room. Nicholas gave Jared yet another assessing glance, as did Alexander, while Michel and Auguste were staring at him in shock.

Michel walked toward him. "She jumped into a lake to rescue a child?"

Jared nodded. "Sure did."

"A book drive?" Auguste echoed.

"The county library was running low. She has a way of making people want to help at the same time she gives a lot of credit, but you've known her a lot longer than I have, so I'm sure you already know that," he said, making a point without the use of his foil. He suspected most of the important points he would make today wouldn't involve his foil.

"You say you gave her fencing lessons," Nicholas said. "What else did you teach Michelina?"

"I hope to believe in herself," Jared said.

"Did you take her to bed?" Michel asked, and a dangerous electricity immediately crackled in the air.

Jared chose his words carefully. "It wouldn't be appropriate for me to discuss something like that with

Michelina's brothers. It should be her choice when and if she discusses that subject."

"I'm her oldest brother," Michel said with a hard glint in his eye. "It's my right to know."

"I'm not arguing with you," Jared said. "It may be your right to know, but it's not my right to tell."

Michel wasn't at all satisfied as he returned to his former position. "Let's resume the match."

They saluted, then began again.

"My brothers and I don't believe you are the right man for Michelina," Michel said. "What would it take to gain your agreement?"

Jared's stomach turned. He had been willing to give the benefit of the doubt to Michelina's brothers. He understood their desire to protect her. She was damn well worth protecting. "I'm not sure what you mean," he said, his foil clashing with Michel's.

"To put it bluntly, how much would it take for you to go away? Permanently," he added, tapping the area just above Jared's heart.

"There isn't enough money," Jared retorted, going on the offensive.

Michel successfully deflected Jared's thrust. "Every man has his price."

"I'm sorry you haven't met one that can't be bought," Jared said, going after him again.

Michel named a sum.

Jared shook his head, fighting his temper, trying to keep his focus on the match.

Michel named a higher sum.

Jared shook his head and took another hit just below his heart.

Michel named a still-higher sum.

Jared's foil clashed with Michel's. "You're wasting your breath. You could offer me all of Marceau, and the answer would be the same."

"You're not good enough for her. She deserves a husband with a title," Michel said. "She'll change her mind and regret being with you."

Unmoved, Jared continued to parry with Michelina's brother.

"You must see that she doesn't know her own mind. She can't be counted on to make such an important—"

Fury raced through Jared, and he turned his foil on Michel with such force that he knocked the prince's weapon out of his hands. His heart hammering a mile a minute, Jared balled his hand into a fist and itched to give Michel what he was asking for.

Instead, he tossed his own foil on the ground. "You can insult me all you want, but lay off your sister. I don't care if you go by Your Majesty, Your Highness, billionaire or brother, if you insult Michelina, then I will cheerfully rip your face off." He pulled off his mask and glove in disgust. "I've had enough of this tea party," he said, and strode toward the changing room.

"Jared," Nicholas called after him.

Taking a deep breath, Jared turned and cocked his head.

"Join us for a beer," he said.

Michel walked toward him. "The duel was a test—unpleasant, but necessary. Michelina is a prize."

"More than you realize," Jared said, the light

dawning as he realized how he'd been set up. He couldn't fault them for wanting to protect her, but it still left a bad taste in his mouth.

"Come, let us make it up to you," Auguste said, extending his hand.

"Please," Alexander said. "Or I'll never hear the end of it from my wife."

Nicholas winced. "Or mine."

Michel gave a heavy sigh. "Or mine."

Jared began to regain a shred of his sense of humor. "Based on how you try to keep Michelina from pursuing any sort of adventure, I would have thought all of you would have chosen utterly docile, agreeable women for your wives."

The Dumont brothers exchanged glances. "It's a fatal flaw among the Dumont men," Nicholas said. "We're drawn to spirited women. But don't laugh," he said, pointing a finger at Jared. "If you've decided to take on Michelina, then you must have the same flaw."

Thirteen

"No, Mother, there is nothing you can say to persuade me to marry Count Ferrar," Michelina said for what felt like the fiftieth time.

"But he would be such an enhancement for Marceau," Queen Anna Catherine said for the fifty-first time. "The advisors are convinced he is the perfect match for you."

Michelina was starting to lose patience. No, that wasn't quite true. She'd had very little patience *before* this meeting had begun. "The advisors are wrong. If they're that crazy about Count Ferrar, then perhaps one of *them* should marry him."

"There's no need to be impertinent," Anna Catherine said with a frown.

"There's no need to continue talking about the count. He's out of the picture."

"Michelina, you've lived a very sheltered life. You should be willing to accept the good advice being offered to you."

Michelina set down her cup of tea. "I'm not as sheltered as I was."

"Your disappearance terrified the entire family," the queen said, and at the drawn expression on her still-lovely face Michelina felt a stabbing pain between her ribs.

"I'm sorry all of you were terrified, but I'm not sorry I disappeared. It gave me a chance to do things I haven't been permitted to do. I learned a lot about myself, about what I want and what I can do."

"And what you think you want is this rancher," her mother said with distaste.

Michelina resented her mother's tone. "I *know* I want him, and I *will* have him."

"You say that as if you have no need to consult your brothers, the advisors or me."

"I don't mind consulting, but it won't change my decision. I'm going to marry Jared, Mother. Nothing will stop me. We can either have the wedding here or in Las Vegas. You choose."

Her mother blinked in disbelief, then shook her head. "This man is totally unprepared to be married to a royal. He has no idea of what is required of you and what will subsequently be required of him."

"Maggie didn't know. Neither did Sophia or Tara."

"Yes, but they're wom—" The queen broke off as if she'd caught herself before making a sexist statement. "Why are you so convinced that this Jared is the right man for you?"

"Because he makes me believe I can do things. He wants me to be true to myself. He loves me, not my position, but he respects my family. Even though I've told him how dysfunctional we are—"

Anna Catherine's eyes widened in horror. "You told him the Dumonts are dysfunctional?"

"Of course. That was why I didn't want to come back. I wanted to go to Vegas, but Jared insisted that we come here because he knew that even though my family can be a pain, you're terribly important to me."

Her mother squeezed the bridge of her nose. "I'm getting too old for this."

Feeling a twist of sympathy for the queen, Michelina reached for her hand. Their relationship had been volatile for years, but she would never forget how her mother had often traded sleep to read to her during her early childhood.

"Mother, whoever I marry has to be strong enough to love me and accept my position. Jared is the strongest man I've ever met."

"But you'll live in Wyoming, of all places!" her mother protested.

"He's going to hire extra help at the ranch so we can come back to Marceau frequently. He thinks our island is beautiful."

"Well, of course he does," Anna Catherine said with pride, then let out a sigh. "I will meet him," she said grudgingly.

"Thank you," Michelina said, bounding around the table and kissing her on the cheek.

The queen gave a start at Michelina's impulsive act of affection. "I'm not promising anything."

"You're going to love him," Michelina promised.

Michelina had been right. The queen had loved Jared. In fact, she thought so much of him that she talked him into building a second, smaller ranch on Marceau with one of the prolific Romeo's superstud offspring. The Marceau ranch served dual purposes. It meant Jared had a reason to visit Marceau and it also provided jobs.

A quickie Vegas wedding was ruled out by everyone except Michelina, but she'd been able to negotiate the one-year engagement her mother had insisted on down to four months. Four months during which she and Jared had not more than fifteen minutes alone. If she'd known her mother had planned such constant supervision, Michelina thought, she would have definitely insisted on Vegas. And she suspected Jared would have been quick to agree.

On the morning of the wedding, the cathedral was packed with dignitaries and celebrities from all over the world. Marceau, Europe, the United States and beyond. The ceremony was being televised by

"You look beautiful." Her brother Michel extended his arm and patted her hand. "You're completely calm," he said, surprise in his voice. "You don't mind this media circus?"

"Jared helped me with it," she said, eager to see her groom. Her heart kept flying into her throat.

"How did he do that?"

"He said if the cameras got too much, just to look at him and remember that we don't have to invite the world into our honeymoon suite."

Michel chuckled. "Thank God for that." He looked at her again, searching her eyes. "You found a good man."

"Yes, I did," she said, still pinching herself at the way her brothers had so quickly accepted Jared into the fold.

"He found a good woman."

The compliment warmed her from the inside out. She couldn't help smiling. "Yes, he did."

The organ began the introduction to "The Wedding March," signaling the time for Michelina to walk down the aisle. "Time to go," she said, so eager she could have skipped instead of walked. She entered the crowded cathedral to the flash of a thousand cameras and the murmured approval of the throng. She saw her brothers in their tuxes on one side and her sisters-in-law in their smaid of gowns, dabbing at tears, on the other sider gaze la hed on to Jared's, and the love she saw in his eyes ove lowed everything else in the ro

Twenty min later, they were r wed hus-band and wife. T hours after that, she ping off his tux in the b oom of a lovely guest he se overlooking the ocean.

"I've been wanting to get you out of these clothes since I first saw you this morning," she said, impatiently shoving down his jacket and tugging at his shirt.

Jared helped by shrugging off his shirt. "It might have provided some interesting film footage if you hadn't been able to restrain yourself from stripping me during the ceremony."

She giggled. "Unforgettable."

"You already are," he told her, lifting his hand to her hair.

She pressed her cheek against his chest and sighed. "Do you realize that I get to spend every single night of my life with you from now on?"

He nodded. "You're stuck."

"You've always told me I can do anything I want to, right?" she asked as she unfastened his slacks and slid her hands inside his briefs; he was already hard.

"Yesss," he hissed, his eyes growing dark with arousal.

"There's something I've wanted to do for a long time," she told him. "But I haven't had the opportunity because there have been too many people around."

"What would that be?" he asked, moaning as she stroked him. "The last time you wanted to do something you haven't done, it involved sexual positions. Michelina, I've been patient, and I somehow managed to deal with the chaperons your mother insisted on, but if you keep rubbing me like that, I can't make any promises about how long I'll last."

"Well, we don't have to do it just once, do we?" she asked, pushing down his briefs and slacks.

Jared swore under his breath.

She pressed an openmouthed kiss to his chest, then slid her tongue down the center of his torso to his belly button. His flat abdomen quivered beneath her attention.

"What are you..."

She lowered her lips still farther, kissing him intimately, taking him into her mouth.

He swore again and again, but his curses of pleasure sounded like music to her ears.

He pulled her slightly away. "*What* are you doing?"

"You've put up with so much insanity for the past four months.... I just wanted to thank you."

"And this is the way you plan to express your gratitude for the rest of our marriage?" he asked, pulling her to her feet.

"Yes."

Jared groaned. "I have just died and gone to heaven." He swept her up in his arms and carried her to the lavish bedroom in the back of the guest house. She would look at the room more closely some other time, when she didn't feel so wanton and needy. As he stripped off her dress, Michelina looked into Jared's eyes and felt herself sinking.

"I know what you do for me," she whispered to him. "You make me believe I can do anything, and you've even promised to help me find Jack now that the wedding craziness is over."

He nodded in agreement.

"What do I do for you?" she continued. He was so strong sometimes it was hard for her to believe that he could need her for anything.

"Besides the obvious…" he said, with a sexy grin that made it difficult for her to breathe. He lifted her hand to his chest, and she felt his heart pound against his rib cage. "You turn a light on inside me. When I'm with you, it never goes out."

And as Michelina sealed her wedding vows with her husband, she knew the light between them would burn forever.

*   *   *   *   *

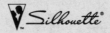

COMING NEXT MONTH

#1519 SCENES OF PASSION—Suzanne Brockmann
Maggie Stanton knew something was missing from her picture-perfect
life, and when she ran into her high school buddy Michael Stone, she
knew just what it was. The former bad boy had grown into a charismatic
man who was everything Maggie had ever dreamed of. But if they were
to have a future together, Maggie would have to learn to trust him.

#1520 CINDERELLA'S MILLIONAIRE—Katherine Garbera
Dynasties: The Barones
Love was the last thing on widower Joseph Barone's mind...until
he was roped into escorting pastry chef Holly Fitzgerald to a media
interview. The brooding millionaire had built an impenetrable wall
around his heart, but delectable Holly was pure temptation. He needed
her—in his bed and in his life—but was he ready to risk his heart again?

#1521 IN BED WITH THE ENEMY—Kathie DeNosky
Lone Star Country Club
ATF agent Cole Yardley didn't believe women belonged in the field,
fighting crime, but then a gun-smuggling investigation brought him and
FBI agent Elise Campbell together. Though he'd intended to ignore Elise,
Cole soon found himself surrendering to the insatiable hunger she stirred
in him....

#1522 EXPECTING THE COWBOY'S BABY—Charlene Sands
An old flame came roaring back to life when Cassie Munroe went home
for her brother's wedding and ran into Jake Griffin, her high school ex.
The boy who'd broken her heart was gone, and in his place was one
sinfully sexy man. They wound up sharing an unforgettable night of
passion that would change Cassie's life forever, for now she was pregnant
with Jake's baby!

#1523 CHEROKEE DAD—Sheri WhiteFeather
Desperate to keep her nephew safe, Heather Richmond turned to
Michael Elk, the man she'd left behind eighteen months ago. Michael
still touched her soul in a way no other man ever had, and she couldn't
resist the seductive promises in his eyes. She only hoped he would
forgive her once he discovered her secret....

#1524 THE GENTRYS: CAL—Linda Conrad
When Cal Gentry went home to his family ranch to recover from the
accident that killed his wife, he found Isabella de la Cruz on his doorstep.
The mysterious beauty needed protecting...and soon found a sense of
security in Cal's arms. Then, as things heated up between them, Cal
vowed to convince Isabella to accept not only his protection, but his
heart, as well.

SDCNM0603